DIAMONDS AND DOOM
The Raven Mysteries

Also by Marcus Sedgwick for older readers

Blood Red, Snow White
The Book of Dead Days
The Dark Flight Down
The Dark Horse
Floodland
The Foreshadowing
The Kiss of Death
Midwinterblood
Revolver
My Swordhand is Singing
She Is Not Invisible
White Crow
Witch Hill

The Raven Mysteries

Flood and Fang
Ghosts and Gadgets
Lunatics and Luck
Vampires and Volts
Magic and Mayhem

Elf Girl and Raven Boy

Fright Forest
Monster Mountains
Scream Sea
Dread Desert

Visit Marcus Sedgwick's website at –
www.marcussedgwick.com

Book 6

MARCUS SEDGWICK

Illustrated by Pete Williamson

Orion
Children's Books

First published in Great Britain in 2011
by Orion Children's Books
Paperback edition first published in Great Britain in 2012
by Orion Children's Books
a division of the Orion Publishing Group Ltd
Orion House
5 Upper St Martin's Lane
London WC2H 9EA
A Hachette UK Company

3 5 7 9 10 8 6 4

Front cover & inside design: www.hereandnowdesign.com

A catalogue record for this book is available from
the British Library.

ISBN 978 1 4440 0348 2

Printed and bound by
CPI Group (UK) Ltd, Croydon, CR0 4YY

www.orionbooks.co.uk

For Lauren

With thanks to Alby

ONE HUNDRED BEST GRAVEYARDS
DR. ARTHUR PELLING
IN ODD WE TRUST
DEAD STORIES

One

From Solstice's completely secret and totally private diary . . .

Dear Diary,

Gasp!

Edgar is missing!

No one has seen him for a whole week. He's not been the same since that business with the bunnies and the cabbages.

I was worried that maybe the whole affair had pushed him too far, and that he'd decided to leave.

I asked Mother and Father about it, and they said that it has happened before. Every twelve years, Edgar goes missing for two weeks, and then turns up again. They call it Edgar's holiday, but oh! Edgar! You can't have a holiday just now, because we need you!

We need you more than ever!

The whole thing is just simply terrible.

I can hardly write it down, it's so awful, but it's true. It seems that we are on the verge of losing our home.

Yes!

The castle itself! I can't bear to think of it!

It began yesterday.

Cudweed and I had been down by the

lake, trying to organise the ducks into having a race, which they simply didn't want to do, and so we'd given up, and decided to come home.

We were walking up the drive to the castle, when we saw an odd thing.

There was a funny little man with a mallet in one hand and a sign in the other. He was using the mallet to bang the sign into the lawn, by the gates to the main road.

The sign said, 'FOR SALE'.

'Hey,' I said. He ignored me.

'Excuse me!' I said a little bit louder and he looked round this time. I didn't like him. I must be learning from Edgar a bit, because I took one look at him and decided I did not like him.

He had a very nasty expression on his face, which was a mixture of being grumpy and very pleased with himself all at the same time.

'What are you doing?' I asked. 'The castle is not for sale.'

'Oh yes it is, sweetie.'

He went on banging the sign into the lawn, and though I tried to get him to explain

himself, he took no notice of us.

'Come on, Cudweed!' I declared rather in a huff. 'Let's go and tell Father about him. He'll soon put a stop to it.'

So we did. We ran all the way up to the castle, which for Cudweed is quite impressive and also quite dangerous, and when we got there, we said, well, I said, because Cudweed was panting so hard, I said, 'Father, there's a man sticking a For Sale sign up in our front garden.'

And he said …

Oh! I can hardly bear to write it down.

He said, 'I know.'

And then he looked grumpy too, but most of all, really, really sad. I'm not sure I've ever seen Father look that sad before, and it worried me.

'But what do you mean?' I asked.

Father just shook his head.

'I mean, I know. It's true. The castle is for sale. We shall have to find somewhere else to live.'

'But why?!' I cried, desperately. I think I might have said Gasp too. Apparently I say that quite a lot. But anyway, 'Why?' I cried.

'Because,' said Father, 'we have no money left. None.'

I stamped my foot. I know it wasn't helpful but I couldn't stop myself.

'I don't believe you!' I said.

Worryingly, Father wasn't even cross with me for speaking so rudely.

'Come with me,' he said to the pair of us,

and we followed him through the castle, down some corridors I'm not sure I've ever seen before, to a very secret place.

The castle treasury. The place where all our money is kept.

Father pulled out a big key from his pocket, and used it to unlock the huge metal door to the treasury.

Inside, it was totally empty.

Not a bean.

Nothing at all in fact, except a thin mouse sitting in the corner, chewing a piece of mouldy toast.

Father sighed.

Mother appeared behind us.

The mouse looked rather fed up at being

disturbed during his dinner.

'Come on, dears,' Mother said. 'It's time to start sorting out what you'll bring with you and what you're going to throw away.'

'Throw away!?' Cudweed and I cried at the same time. 'Why do we have to throw anything away?!'

'Because dears,' said Mother, 'wherever it is we end up, our new house, I mean, it's not going to be quite as big as this one. In fact, you should probably just pack one suitcase. Between you.'

Well, Cudweed and I were really upset then.

'But why don't you have any more money?' Cudweed asked.

'Because we spent it all,' explained Mother. 'This place costs a fortune to run. And the way we get through servants! The bill for Box and Sons last month alone was enormous.'

'But,' I said, 'But ... But ... Can't you do one of those things that grown-ups do? Like go to a bank and borrow money? Or something?'

Then Father gave us a very long and confusing explanation of how he had already done that. He'd actually already sold the castle to the bank, so that they gave us a big lot of money, which we have then been paying back to them in order to rent the castle from them each month and to live on and buy servants with, and how now there isn't any left. At all.

I was very confused.

'So, the bank owns the house?'

Father nodded.

'Not us?'

He shook his head.

'And now they're selling it?'

He nodded again.

'Who to?'

'To whoever wants to buy it,' Mother said. 'Now go and tidy your rooms, dears, because there are some people coming to look at it this afternoon.'

And they did.

The people I mean.

They came to look at Castle Otherhand, and I hated them, but what I hate most is that Edgar isn't here to help us. And by the time he gets back, even if it is next week, it might all be too late.

By then, Castle Otherhand might have been sold.

Oh!

Gasp!

There's something else.

Last night, as I went to sleep thinking evil thoughts about the people who want to buy our house, I thought Edgar had come back.

I heard a noise at the window, and sat up, and there was Edgar sitting on the other side of the glass.

At least I thought it was, but suddenly I realised it was too small to be Edgar.

I went over to the window, and to my very great surprise, saw a small, young raven sitting there.

I expected him to fly away, but when I opened the window, he popped straight in to my room and sat on my head.

I lifted him down and sat him on my wrist, which is a much better place for a raven to sit.

'Who are you?' I asked, and then I noticed an eeny-weeny tag tied to his ankle. ROB THE RAVEN, it said.

'Rob?' I asked.

The little bird looked up at me.

'**Erk!**' he said.

'Well I never,' I said.

So now we have a new raven in the castle, but not the raven that we really need right now.

Rob the Raven

Edgar! Come back! Please!

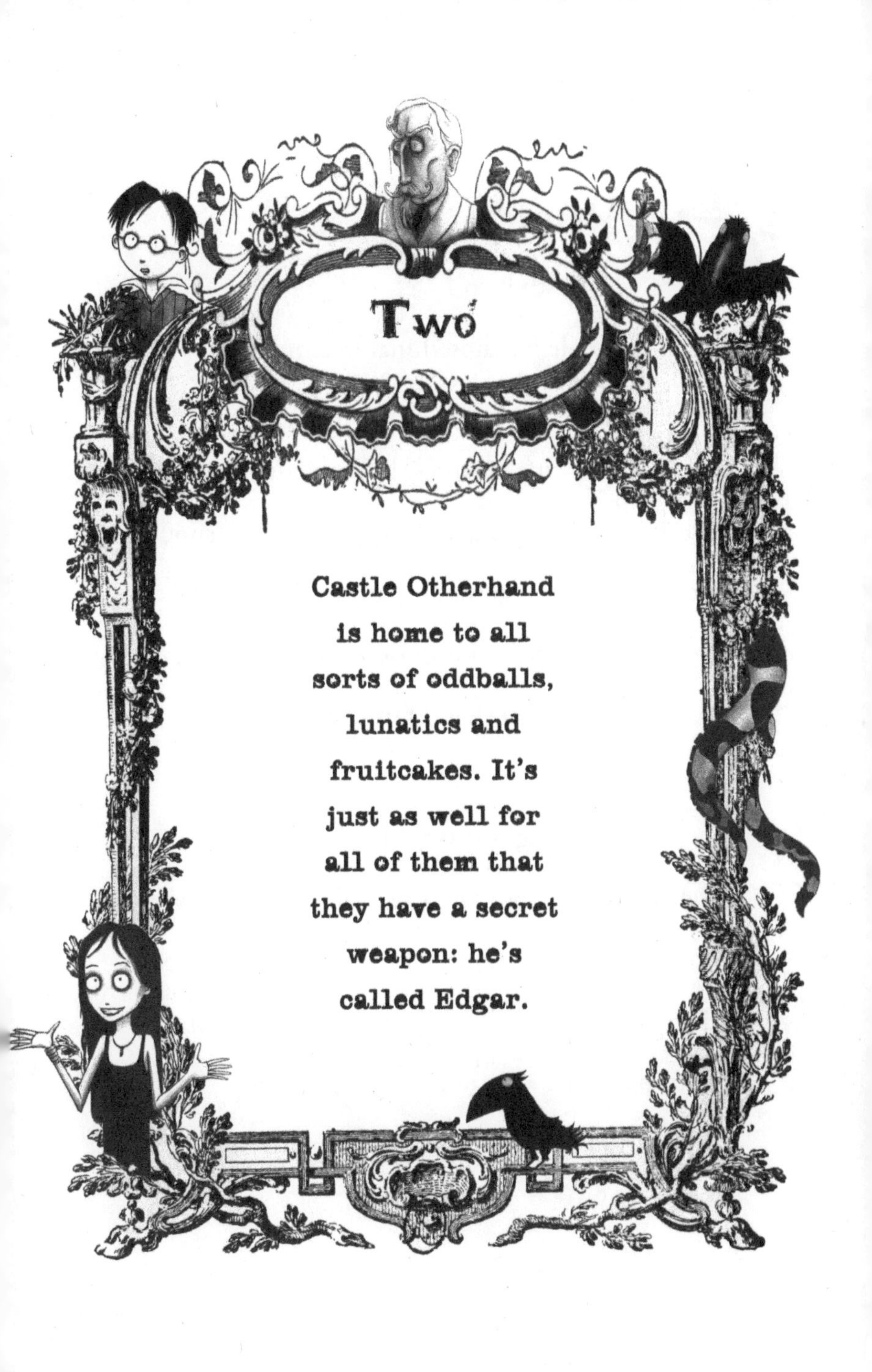

Two

Castle Otherhand is home to all sorts of oddballs, lunatics and fruitcakes. It's just as well for all of them that they have a secret weapon: he's called Edgar.

Rurk!!!

Honestly!

You leave those lunatics alone for five minutes, and when you get back, it's a madhouse.

I say five minutes. It was actually two weeks, but you get my point. Two weeks should not be long enough to get into serious bother, but then I suppose, I'd underestimated the ability of the Otherhand family to cause chaos and catastrophe.

I'd thought it would be safe to leave them for a fortnight, but anyway, I didn't have any choice. I had to keep a very special appointment. They call it Edgar's Holiday in the castle, but it's nothing of the sort, no!

I have to attend a very important

gathering of ravens from across the land. Sometimes there's twelve years between the meetings, sometimes longer, depending on how grumpy we're feeling. Ravens from north, south, east and west, from big houses and castles, from remote mountaintops and deep forests. We all get together to discuss Important Raven Business. What's been going on, what needs sorting out, who's been rude to whom. That kind of thing. And if, in the process, we eat and drink a little bit more than normal, well, that's no one else's business, is it?

In fact, on the last night of my holiday, by which I mean, Very Important Raven Business, I had had maybe one or two more morsels to eat than I should have done.

So I was a very fat and flappy bird that flew lazily home, expecting to return to a sleepy castle, with absolutely nothing odd, or dangerous, or smelly going on at all.

As it turned out, I was wrong, and the first thing that happened quite put my beak out.

Ark!

All looked well as I flapped up the valley

towards the castle, gliding on warm drafts of air where I could, because I was feeling very chubby and rather tired.

I thought I'd stop by the Red Room first, and then find somewhere nice and cosy to have a sleep.

My route happened to take me past Solstice's bedroom window.

I was so shocked by what I saw inside that I flew straight into the wall opposite.

I think I chipped my beak. But my feathers were in even more of a flap because of what made me fly into the wall in the first place.

Which was this: I had seen something most bothersome.

Hardly believing my eyes, I recovered my senses enough to fly back around to her window where I perched on the ledge.

The window was shut, or I'd have barged straight in, but there was Solstice, and sitting on her delicate little wrist, was a small, but undeniably real little raven. A ravenlet, in fact. Not just one of those stuffed ones that Minty once made to try and sell, but a real one.

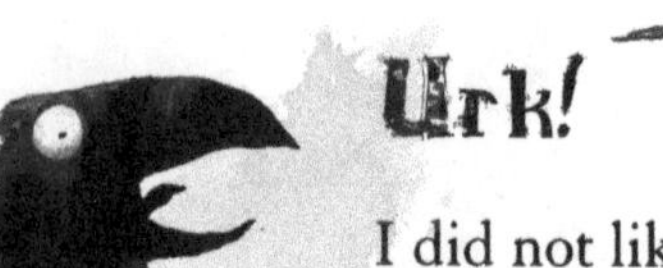

I did not like what I saw.

She was tickling it under the chin.

And the precocious little bird was flapping and

squawking and generally being all nice and cute

and …

Urk!

She tickled it again. Well that was it. I nearly shattered the window I banged it with my beak so hard, but I'd forgotten about flying into the wall, and now my beak hurt twice as much.

Solstice looked over.

'Edgar!' she cried, though it was a bit muffled through the glass. She came over and let me in. 'Edgar! You're back! Where have you been?'

'**Rurk**,' I declared. I admit I was in a very bad mood already, what with being tired and fat, flying into a wall and then seeing this young upstart being coo-cooed at by Solstice. Of all people, she should know better than to canoodle with a strange bird.

'Are you all right, Edgar?' Solstice said. 'Your beak looks a little ...'

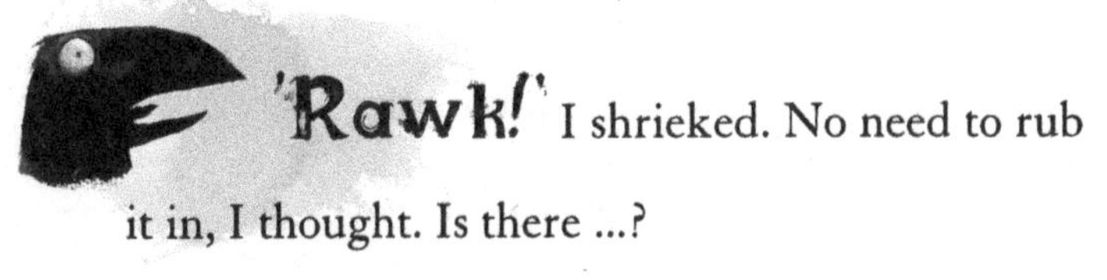

'**Rawk!**' I shrieked. No need to rub it in, I thought. Is there ...?

Solstice changed the conversation. Nice idea, wrong subject.

'Edgar, look!' she cooed. 'We have a new friend in the castle. A little bird. Another raven! Isn't that wonderful?'

The little impostor looked at me and flapped his feathers.

'**Erk**,' he said.

'Oh, Edgar,' Solstice gushed, 'I think he likes you!'

I said nothing.

Cheeky bounder. Sneaking in to my castle when I wasn't looking and …

'Edgar, aren't you going to say hello?' said Solstice. 'His name's Rob.'

Rob indeed. I ask you. Rob the Raven. So his name alliterates. Very clever.

'Erk!' piped up the ravenlet, with what I assume was supposed to be a friendly look on his face.

'Edgar …' said Solstice, sternly. 'Play nicely.'

I thought about that for a long time.

Then, 'Urrrrk,' I said, very quietly.

'That's better,' said Solstice. 'We're going to get on famously. At least … at least … we could have done, but now … !'

At this point she burst into tears.

I was so surprised, I didn't know what to do. But little Rob the Raven did. He bounded into Solstice's hair and began to nibble her ear!

Honestly!

But Solstice wasn't listening.

'Oh!' she wailed. 'It's true, Edgar. We're going to lose the castle! We've run out of money, and we're going to have to leave.'

'**Erk**,' said Rob.

Limited vocabulary, I thought. Let me show him.

'Futhork – rark – rurk!'

I cried.

Which meant, as anyone who knows the first thing about ravens can tell you, oh no we're not, not if I, Edgar the brave and fearless raven, have anything to do with it!

But deep inside, I didn't feel so sure about this one.

Money's not really my thing, you see.

Three

The castle once
had a pair of
cats, called Tibbs
and Willow.
Unfortunately,
Cudweed fed
them so much
they were soon
renamed Tubbs
and Wallow.

I decided to go and see what on earth was going on, even though that meant leaving Solstice with Rob the Ravenlet.

'You'll go and make everything better, won't you, Edgar?' she said. I've got little Rob to look after me.'

On which note, Rob snuffled in Solstice's hair in what was probably supposed to be a really charming way.

I gave the small piece of black cheekiness a very severe look.

'**Erk**,' he chirped happily.

I thought about attacking him but I could see that Solstice wouldn't approve, so I decided to bide my time and left them to it.

As I left Solstice's room I heard her coo

once more at Rob.

'Oh, that is soooo charming,' she said.

And then she giggled.

I felt my blood starting to boil, so I cooled down with a big swoop across the Great Courtyard into the Small Hall by the back door.

Where I found an extraordinary sight.

A teetering tower of boxes stood in the Hall, and a stream of servants from the stairs and

each and every doorway was carrying more and more boxes to add to the pile.

Minty and Valevine stood, arm in arm, watching the scene.

It worried me. Minty and Valevine. Arm in arm. Most odd.

I thought I'd see what everyone else was up to, and, heading for Cudweed's room, I passed a small crowd of people in the Dining Room, and by which I mean, not *castle* people, but *other* people.

Strangers.

One of them, a man I took an instant dislike to, was holding a clipboard and pointing at various things around the room.

'And that is believed to be a fifteenth-

century soup tureen,' he was saying about a dented fruit bowl Minty had bought last summer in a yard sale.

Someone saw me flying by and squeaked.

'Oh! The place isn't infested with vermin, is it? I should think that should take another few thousand off the price!'

The man with the clipboard said something to make me hate him even more.

'Oh, don't worry. Any sign of creatures in the castle will be sorted by pest control before you, or whoever buys the castle, takes ownership …'

Pest control!?

The only pests that needed controlling were carrying clipboards as far as I was concerned.

I dive-bombed!

Maybe I am carrying a little, ahem, excess weight at the moment, because normally I would have been able to swoop down, get in a couple of deadly pecks, and get out again, unscathed.

But what actually happened was I got my angles a bit wrong, missed the man, hit a lady standing next to him, and then got a sharp slap on my behind from a large wooden clipboard.

'Ugh!' screamed the woman. 'Nasty thing!'

'I'll get him this time,' swore the clipboard

man, taking another swipe at me.

Well, I was out of there, nursing my pride and my stinging backside, before he could do permanent damage.

I was in seven shades of fuss by the time I got to Cudweed's room. The door was open and I was just in time to see Solstice and Rob saunter in.

Minty and Valevine were there too.

Valevine was looking at Rob.

'Edgar!' he declared. He peered in closely. 'Have you shrunk?'

Well that was it. The last straw.

I went ballistic. I flapped and flew about the room like a firework bouncing off the inside of a box, squawking like my passport had got lost in the post the day before a holiday. A *real* holiday.

Then I flew into a wall again, and fell onto my back on an old armchair.

I decided not to move, and lay still, staring at the ceiling.

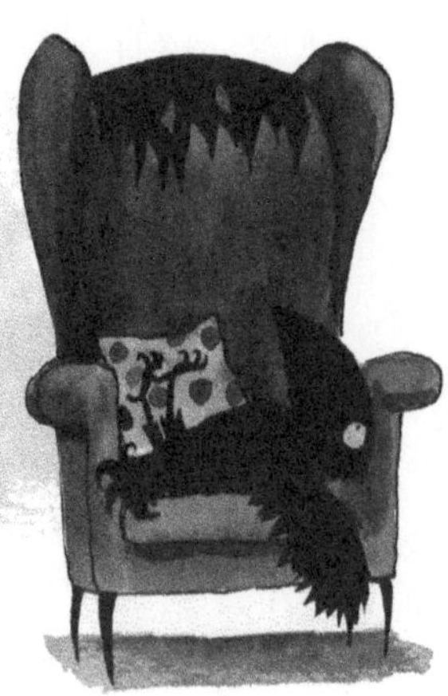

'I'm worried about Edgar,' Solstice said.

'Never mind that,' Minty said. 'I thought I told you two to start packing. Cudweed, we now see, has done precisely nothing, and you, Solstice, what have you done?'

Solstice hesitated.

'A bit less than Cudweed,' she admitted

quietly.

'Well, it's got to stop!' Valevine roared. 'Or rather, it's got to start! The packing! There's a very good chance that one of those people downstairs is going to buy our castle, and then we'll be out of here in no time at all. So get cracking! Ha! And packing! Ha ha! Oh, and Solstice, who is this bird?'

Solstice sighed sadly.

'He's called Rob, and I don't know where he came from but I'm keeping him. Even if we do have to move. Isn't he cute, Mother?'

Minty ignored this. I approved.

'Children. Start packing immediately! Do you hear? Immediately!'

I did not approve of that, and as soon as

Lord and Lady Otherhand shut the door behind them, it appeared that neither did Solstice, nor Cudweed.

'I simply shan't,' announced Solstice.

'Coo,' said Cudweed. 'But what can we do?'

'Well,' said Solstice. 'The reason that we have to leave is because the castle is for sale, yes?'

Cudweed nodded sadly.

'And the reason it's for sale is because we have no money, right?'

'Right.'

'So, if we were suddenly to find a lot of money, a very large lot of money, I mean, then we could buy the castle ourselves and everything would be all right. Right?'

Cudweed nodded again, wide-eyed.

'But where are we going to find a vast and ridiculous amount of money?' he asked.

'I've been thinking,' Solstice said. 'It's about time we found the fabulous lost treasure of Castle Otherhand.'

'But we've tried that before,' Cudweed protested. 'Hundreds of people have.'

'Yes,' agreed Solstice. 'But we found one bit of it, didn't we? When there was all that business with our hairy teacher and that cursed diamond. So the rest of it must exist! And I've got an idea…'

And what an idea it turned out to be.

Who was to know, at that moment, what disaster and total doom it was to take us all towards?

Doom!

When what we needed was diamonds!

Four

The fabulous lost treasure, the result of centuries of pillaging and plundering, was actually hidden by the Defreeques, the castle's previous owners ...

Unfortunately, there was no time to put Solstice's plan into operation that evening, for Minty arrived soon afterwards and did two things.

First, she had what can only be described as a screaming fit, because Cudweed and Solstice had still not started packing, and secondly, she announced it was bedtime.

All in all it was a pretty sour end to what had already been a pretty rotten day.

I had trouble sleeping that night.

Perched in my old brass cage in the Red Room, I swung back and forth, worrying about

our future. When I did get to sleep, I had strange and bothering dreams, nightmares of the many weird and dangerous things that had ever happened in the castle: attacks by monstrous beasts, ghosts, werewolves, vampires and so on and so forth. And then I had even stranger and more bothersome nightmares about things that had never happened … but that might.

These things were very, very, very odd indeed, and I struggled to even put words to what I saw, but nevertheless, I was terrified.

In the wee small hours of the morning, before the sun came up, I still couldn't sleep, and decided to take to the valley for a spin.

'Urk!' I grumbled as I lazily flapped out of the Red Room, and sat for a moment on the stone balustrade of the High Terrace. I stretched my wings. They were stiff and achy.

I felt unbelievably old.

My mood, to put it simply, was stinky.

In the soft weak grey light, I surveyed the old castle, my home for many years, and the valley below it, the mountains above.

Could it be true that I would have to leave all this behind?

I tilted off the wall and stretched my wings, swooping down across the lawns and the lake, and then began a slow and steady climb into the high air.

As I did, the dawn rose, and I flew to

meet it. Suddenly a strong golden light burst across the horizon and, just as suddenly, I realised something.

It was this. I've seen many generations of Otherhands come and go, and before that, a few centuries of Defreeques, and it has never once occurred to me that my home is anywhere other than this valley and this castle, no matter who owns it, or what it's called.

And yet, as I contemplated the fact that the Otherhands, this current particularly crazy bunch of Otherhands, might very soon have to leave the place, I knew that I could not stay behind without them.

I would have to go with them.

Why? Well, because, I think, that is to say, urk, I, aaark, love them. Yes, with all their weird and wonderful ways, even stroppy old Valevine, I love them all.

I felt odd. Maybe I'd eaten something even more rotten than usual.

But as I flapped on, I could not deny it.

I loved them all. Well, apart from Nanny Lumber, that is, obviously.

A small bead of moisture crept to the corner of my eye, but I'm sure it was just the cold morning wind making me cry, and nothing else.

Umm.

I flew on and, lost in these strange thoughts, I was startled when I realised there was something flying next to me.

I turned my head to see that young upstart, Rob the Really Charming Raven, madly beating his little wings alongside me.

I ignored him.

'Erk!' he said.

Really. I ask you.

'Erk!' he cried again. More insistently this time, but I still ignored him.

'ERK!' he squeaked.

Now, I don't want to take up too much of your time translating raven speech, but let me explain that what Rob was saying was basically this: I really think you ought to come to the castle and see what Solstice and Cudweed are doing because I don't think they should be but I haven't been here that long so maybe you ought to come instead because you probably know more about this kind of thing than I do. Probably. Please.

If you're wondering how '**Erk**' can mean all that, well, let's just say that we ravens have to make a little go a long way.

Anyway, I ignored him again.

Then he pecked me on the head, mid-air, just like that.

I turned to peck him back, but he fled for the castle, and so I chased him all the way home, determined not to let the little rascal get away with it.

But by the time I got there, I had completely forgotten why I was chasing him, and anyway, it seemed Rob was right.

Solstice and Cudweed were up to something.

Five

Edgar hasn't always been so grumpy. He can't actually remember a time where he was less grumpy, but considers that his grumpiness is the only logical response to the family known as the Otherhands.

Yes.

Up to something. I knew this immediately.

For one thing, it was way too early in the morning for Solstice and Cudweed to be awake and, apparently, functioning. They usually get up at the crack of eleven or so, at the earliest, but here they were, not long after sun-up, reading.

This was another clue, for although Solstice can often be found reading, it is not something Cudweed makes much of a habit of. Yet, here they were, tucked away in a tiny room on the fourth floor of the north wing, poring over a large and heavy-looking book.

The third and final clue was that when I flapped noisily into the room, with Rob behind me, they slammed the book shut, sprang to their

feet, and cried,

'We didn't do anything!'

and,

'It wasn't me!'

Maybe not,

I thought, or rather,

not yet.

When they saw it was me, however, Solstice sat down again and picked up the book.

'Oh Edgar,' she said. 'You made me jump. And we have work to do.'

'Gark?' I said. Is that so?

'Yes,' she stated. 'We have to save the castle.'

Tell me something I don't know, I thought.

'And this is how we're going to do it.

With this.'

Aha! It was one of Minty's spell books, and all of a sudden, I got the picture. She was going to try and cast a spell to find the treasure.

'Erk,' said Rob, settling down on the arm of the big old sofa on which Solstice was sitting.

Immediately she tickled him under the chin.

'Don't worry, Rob. It's perfectly safe. It's such a good idea of mine, and everything's going to be all right.'

Now, taking those statements in reverse order, I did not for one minute agree that everything was going to be all right, nor that it was a good idea to mess about with Minty's old spell books. And finally, as for it being safe … well, I am

reminded of the time when Solstice was young, and just learning to read, and one day found a 'funny big old book' of her mother's to practise with.

It took us weeks to put the castle straight afterwards. Total and utter carnage would be a mild description of what happened.

So you can understand why I didn't leap to support this latest idea of Solstice's.

'**Erk**,' said Rob. I told you so. Didn't I tell you so?

That's what he meant, but I wasn't going to give it to him that easily.

Instead, I had this to say to Solstice.

'Rurk!'

But she ignored me, and she and Cudweed began hunting through the book again.

'There must be the right kind of spell in here somewhere,' Cudweed said, then added, 'And is it breakfast time yet?'

'Just as soon as we find the right spell,' his sister said, sternly.

'Well, hurry up then,' Cudweed moaned.

So, they looked through all kinds of spells. Ones to make people thinner, ones to make frogs dance, ones to turn sugar into mud. All sorts in fact, but by the time they had flicked through the whole book, they had not found a spell to locate lost treasure.

Solstice sighed.

'Well,' she said, 'There's one more book to look through.'

'Fine,' said Cudweed, 'but in that case, I am going to the kitchen to get some breakfast to have while we do it.'

Solstice sighed again, but she knew better than to get between Cudweed and food.

'Be quick about it,' was all she said. 'And bring it back here so no one knows you're up. Right?'

While Cudweed was gone, Solstice began to read through the last book, sighing and muttering, flicking through the pages, while somehow still managing to tickle Rob under his beak the whole time.

Cudweed came back, munching a croissant so filled with strawberry jam it looked like it might explode. Fatally and messily.

'Oh, Cudweed!' Solstice said unhappily. 'I still haven't found anything. None of them are what we need.'

The book lay open on a spell to summon a cow missing in the mountains.

Solstice was quiet for a long time.

Cudweed spoke through a mouthful of bun and jam, slurping orange juice as he did so.

'Um, mmm um fum, um, um fum um?' he said.

'Pardon me?'

'Um um fum, mum. Mum um fum um mum.'

'Oh!' said Solstice. 'I see what you mean!'

She does?! I thought.

'Um fum um, mum mum, fum um,' said Cudweed. 'Fum.'

'So what you mean is, why don't we use the cow summoning spell?'

'Um fum.'

'And just change the words a bit. Yes?'

'Fum,' said Cudweed, spraying me with bits of croissant. He began picking them off my feathers and popping them in his mouth. I flew off in disgust, but Solstice was already getting excited about the idea.

'Yes! What a plan!' she said. 'Great idea!

Cudweed, you are a genius! What can possibly go wrong?'

Do I really need to answer that, I wondered, but I said nothing. I tried a bit of croissant and jam that was sticking to my foot.

Disgusting.

'Here, Cudweed,' Solstice said, giving him the book. 'You read the spell, and I'll do the actions and find the ingredients and what not. We'll be saved in no time!'

Yes, I thought, saved.

Either that, or indescribably, bafflingly, dead.

Six

High on the hillside above the castle is a folly; a miniature castle built by the third Lord Otherhand as a place to sit and think. No one goes there now. It smells.

Not long after that, around the time that Cudweed would normally be having second breakfast, the spell-making was done.

The result was, in a word, uneventful.

Not much seemed to have changed or happened. In fact, it seemed that nothing had happened at all.

There hadn't been very many ingredients for the spell. A couple of slippers and the ear of a donkey was about it. Otherwise, it had involved quite a few long words, many of which Cudweed was unable to say properly, which meant that Solstice kept having to tell him, which meant that Cudweed got cross, which led to some fuss. That was how Cudweed's orange juice got spilled across the spell book.

After some mopping, they had continued, and now Solstice and Cudweed were just moping.

They sat staring into space.

'Well,' said Solstice. 'That's it. We may as well go and start packing our stuff. We did our best, and we failed. Nothing for it but to admit defeat and start sorting things for the charity shops.'

Cudweed was chewing a bacon sandwich, enthusiastically. He always gets hungrier when he gets worried.

'Are you sure the spell didn't work?' he asked. 'Maybe right now the treasure of Otherhand is sitting in the Small Hall, or the Dining Room, or even your bedroom, just waiting to be picked up.'

Solstice's face brightened.

'Yes, I suppose you're right. After all, we didn't know exactly which bits of the cow-finding spell to change. Maybe the treasure has appeared in the barn by the kitchen garden! Come on, let's go and see! But first, we'd better put all the books back where they came from.'

So they did.

First they staggered through the castle with armfuls of books, and then we set off outside.

I followed, eager to see if they'd saved us all. Rob came too, which made me realise something else that had been niggling at my mind.

Solstice was obviously thinking the same thing.

'Cudweed?' she asked, as they trotted

towards the gardens. 'Where's Fellah?'

'Ah, well, I'm glad you asked me that,' said Cudweed. 'As it happens, I thought that in case the spell didn't work. And I mean just in case, because I'm sure it has, that I would leave Fellah to start my packing. I started him on sorting my clothes into black and grey piles…'

Solstice raised an eyebrow.

'Good idea, brother,' she said uncertainly. 'Good, er, idea.'

I could only imagine the levels of mess that would result from leaving Cudweed's monkey to his own devices in the boy's already messy bedroom.

Cudweed seemed happy enough however, so we forgot about the primate for the time being.

Instead, we came to the barn by the kitchen garden, where we found … absolutely nothing.

So we checked the Small Hall, the Dining Room, the Kitchens … in short we hunted round all of the castle, well, every bit where Valevine and Minty weren't. And it was fair to assume that had the treasure materialised in some place where they were, then the screams of joy would have been heard from one end of the valley to the other.

Finally, we ended up in Solstice's bedroom. Still nothing, and now the pair were absolutely miserable.

'That IS it,' Cudweed said, and Solstice

could only nod in agreement.

Then that pesky little new boy, Rob, hopped onto her wrist.

'**Erk**,' he said, in what was meant to be a really cute way.

'Oh, well,' said Solstice, 'at least we have Rob. He's really cute.'

Now, I have to confess that at that point, something flipped inside my noodle, and I felt cross, grumpy, and generally very sulky indeed.

I flapped away without another word, leaving them to it.

Hah!

Those Otherhands could rot as far as I was concerned. That was what I tried to tell myself but, in fact, as I'd realised only that morning, I did love them after all, and could not be separated from them.

Now, I don't know if you've ever tried to sulk at someone you really like, but it's actually very hard, and that made me even grumpier. I mean, there you are, trying to be sulky, and all that happens is that you keep feeling sorry for them instead. How irritating!

I flapped round the castle in a really stinky mood, unable even to decide which of my favourite sulking spots to choose. I know why that was. At the back of my small bird brain was the thought that any spot I chose might be the very last spot I ever sulked in.

I came to the Great Hall, and found Minty. She was in deep discussion with the man with the clipboard!

Rark!

'Yes, Mr Binkum,' she was saying. 'I understand that the castle is a little dusty, but we are doing our best to make it attractive to buyers. But it's awfully hard. The place is enormous and we can't afford any more staff at the moment. If we could we wouldn't need to leave, would we?'

She tried to give a weak smile, but Mr Binkum wasn't impressed.

'Mrs Otherhand,' he said, which put a withering frown on Lady Otherhand's face, 'I think you ought to

know that we are doing our best to market and sell this … unusual property of yours. Dust is one thing, but pests are quite another!'

Here, the blasted man point at me! At me!

Ark! I squawked.

'If,' continued Mr Binkum, 'you actually want to sell this place, I suggest you get the wildlife removed first! I shall return at two o'clock. I have three families to view the castle. Good day!'

Minty was dumbfounded.

I flew down to see if I could cheer her up. I meant to land on her shoulder, but I landed on her head accidentally.

'Oh Edgar!' she cried. 'DO get off! Not now. Can't you see the mess we're in!'

Unwanted again, I skulked away to find somewhere to sulk, then remembered that that was what I'd been trying to do in the first place. And got even crosser.

'Futhork,' I stated, as bold as you please, and in the end, I found myself lying on an armchair in the Red Room, gazing into space.

Quite the suicidal bird I was, just then.

The door opened.

Solstice came in, and sat on the arm of the chair.

'Edgar,' she said quietly.

My beak remained firmly closed. I stared at a tear in the wallpaper.

'Edgar, dear,' she continued, 'I think I have realised something, something a bit sensitive. I think I may have upset you. Is that right, Edgar?'

I decided to say nothing.

'Edgar, are you jealous? Of Rob? Are you jealous of Rob the Raven?'

I said nothing for a very long time, then, as quietly as quiet I gave one tiny little noise.

'Erk,' I said.

'Oh, Edgar,' Solstice cried, 'I'm sorry. I have been mean and rotten and you know that I think you're the very best bird in the whole world. Don't you? Don't you, Edgar?'

Then she kissed the top of my head, and I blushed beneath my black feathers, and all in all, I felt much better. In fact I felt quite happy.

Blast the girl.

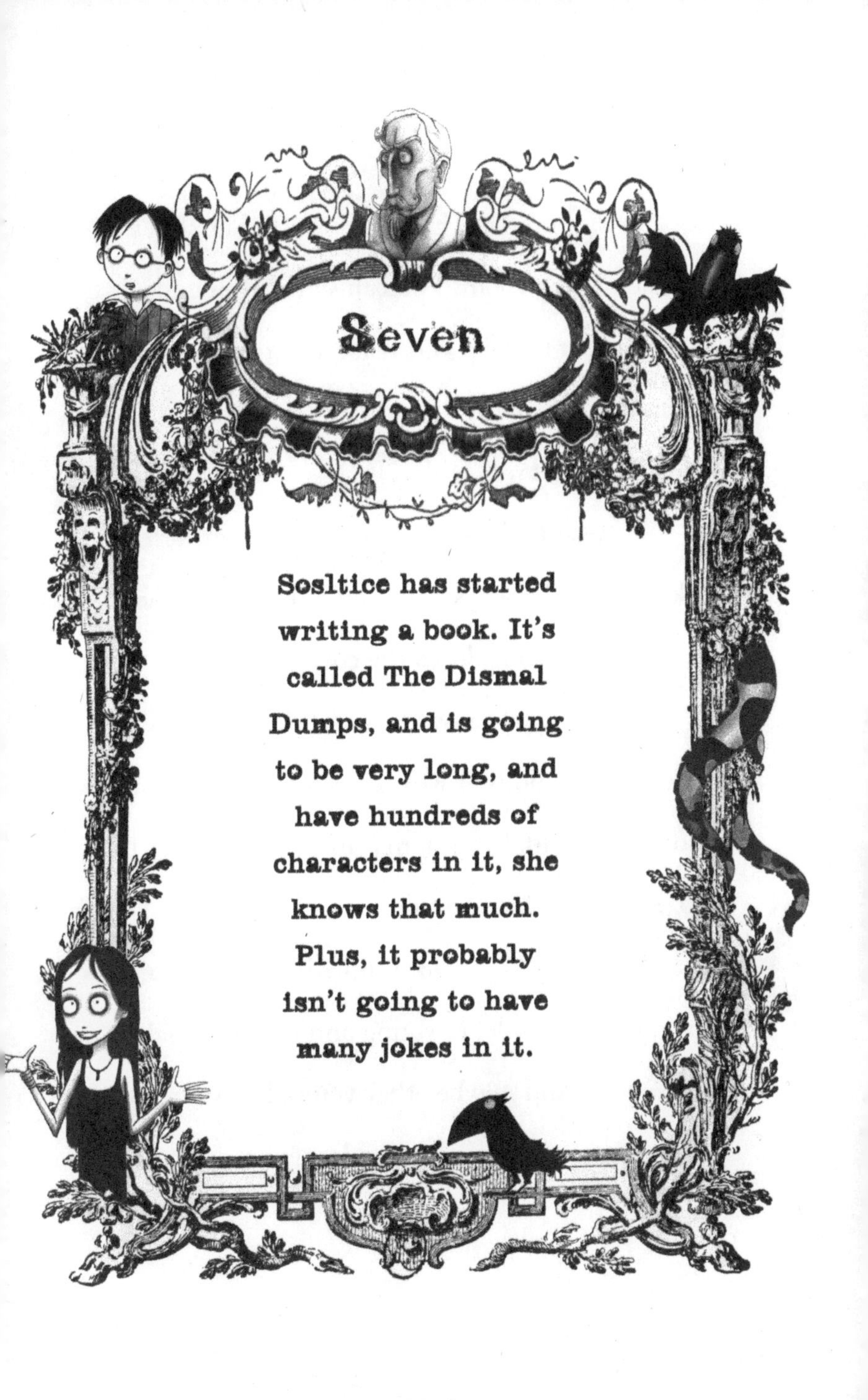

Seven

Sosltice has started writing a book. It's called The Dismal Dumps, and is going to be very long, and have hundreds of characters in it, she knows that much. Plus, it probably isn't going to have many jokes in it.

'Come on, Edgar,' Solstice said. 'Let's go back to my room. You can start helping me decide what to keep and what to throw out. Would that be okay?'

'**Urk**,' I said.

'Good,' she said. 'If we have to go, at least I know I will always have you to look after me.'

We set off down the corridor.

'And you know, Edgar, I don't think you need to be jealous of Rob. He's nice, and he could do with an old, I mean, mature, raven to look up to. A role model, you know?'

'**Ark!**' I said. I quite liked the idea of being a role model to young and impressionable ravenlets. And maybe other young birds too. Of course, it would mean being less grumpy on the whole. Hmm. Tricky one.

I decided to give it some thought.

'**Kark**,' I said, and left it at that.

'And we'd better make some progress with packing this morning,' Solstice added, 'because there are more people coming to see the castle this afternoon.'

'**Rurk**,' I agreed.

As we walked, memories flooded in from all sides. Most of them concerning the unlikely and yet spectacularly unpleasant deaths of servants all over the castle.

Ahh. Happy days. And now, in fact, the question of servants was a particularly pressing one. Minty had just let the last remaining servants go, since there was nothing to pay them with except cabbages, left over from Valevine's crazy experiments.

Never had Castle Otherhand seen so little life. Apart from Cook, Flinch and Nanny Lumber, there was one solitary servant called Pete, though he spent more of his time sketching in a notebook than servanting, and one kitchen boy called James. Even Nanny Lumber was out of action, laid up in bed with a case of nose-rot.

With no money left in the coffers, there was no one else to help with the running of the castle, except Spatchcock the gardener. He hadn't been seen inside since that business with the fang beast, after which he had declared that the castle was far too dangerous, and he'd stick to the rhubarb patch in future.

Progress on packing the castle up was very, very slow.

We saw Valevine and Flinch carrying a box, but they were carrying it the wrong way. Not out of the lab and down the stairs to the Small Hall, but up the stairs instead.

'Shouldn't you be taking that the other way?'

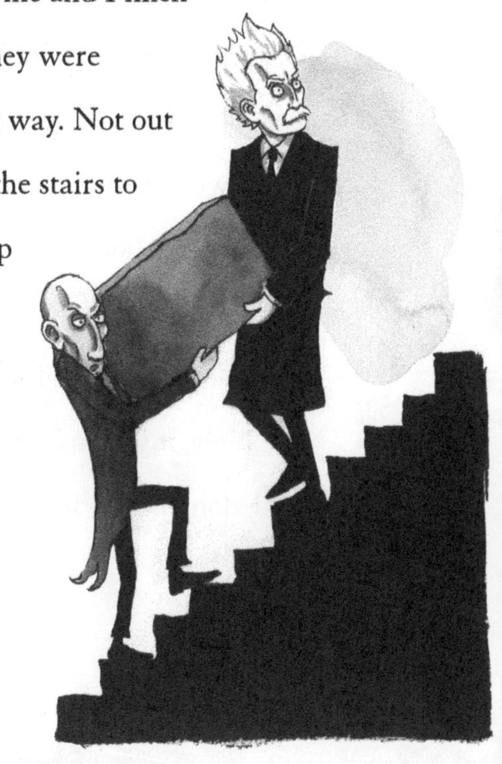

Solstice called to her father.

'Ha!' cried Valevine. 'You would think so, wouldn't you? But no! This is not packing! This is something for my new invention!'

'But Father, we don't have time for you to do any more inventing. We have to pack, and we need everyone's help.'

'Aha! And what better thing to help us pack, than an automatic packing machine? Come on, Flinch, let's get this lot up to the lab and then we can really get cracking!'

Solstice shook her head, but was too miserable to argue.

'We can't even fail properly,' was all she said.

Now, it was just around then, as we walked along the wide gallery that runs from the back of the gallery above the Small Hall to the rest of the castle, that I noticed an odd thing.

I noticed that it was snowing.

Nothing odd there, you might think, and I would have agreed with you but for one thing. It was snowing inside.

At the time, I was feeling so gloomy, that I didn't pay much attention.

I pecked Solstice gently on her shoulder to get her to notice, but all she said was, 'Oh, Edgar, I'm fed up too.'

Maybe the roof needed fixing, I thought. It's probably snowing outside, and the roof needs mending.

And the fact that the room in which it was snowing was on the first floor, and that there were lots of floors above it, didn't seem to enter my brain, nor did the fact that it might just have made sense if it were the winter, when, in fact, it was summertime.

But if I didn't notice that weirdness, none of us could fail to notice the weirdness that very soon began to take over the whole castle, making indoor snow seem very normal indeed.

Eight

Solstice has a crush on the lead singer of teen-emo-screamo-speed-goth-metal band, I Was Born Wrong. He's called Creepy Chris and Solstice thinks he's completely handsome.

'Let's go and see how Cudweed's getting on first,' suggested Solstice.

With a monkey sorting his stuff? Not very well, I suspected, but at least it was an excuse not to start Solstice's own packing.

We heard the noise three corridors before we got there. As we approached Cudweed's room, it got worse.

We opened the door to find a scene more disastrous than you would think possible. It appeared that Fellah the monkey, let loose in Cudweed's wardrobe, had gone utterly loopy.

He was leaping and screeching his way around the room, dressed, sort of, in some of Cudweed's clothes, the rest of which were sprayed

round the room as though a stick of dynamite had been set off in the boy's wash basket.

Cudweed was making a vain and vague attempt to get Fellah to calm down, but it was as if the monkey was drunk on jolly-juice, for not only would he not calm down, but the moment he saw me, he screeched like a rusty train and hurled himself at me.

I was not quick enough, and in a moment, the smelly beast was on me, with teeth and nails and noise assaulting every poor black feather on my body.

Solstice shrieked, Cudweed wailed and I could do nothing but start saying my prayers, for, though I hate to admit it, the monkey is actually much stronger than me.

'Nooo!' cried Solstice, and all of a sudden, I was aware of something else.

Rob had arrived in Cudweed's bedroom, and seeing the scene, immediately began pecking the monkey's skull for all he was worth. I think the shock of being attacked when he thought he was the one doing the attacking was

enough to get Fellah to stop.

He let go of me and I bolted for a high wardrobe to recover, from where I saw Rob continue his abuse of the odious ape. I was impressed, I have to say. Rob was fast. So fast, in fact, that Fellah could not grab him, try though he might. Every swipe and swoop he made for the little ravenlet ended in failure, and it was all he could do ward off the repeated pecking that Rob was inflicting on him.

In the end, Fellah cowered in a corner while Rob darted at him like a tiny black feathery guided missile. I almost felt sorry for the monkey.

But only almost, obviously.

Only then did Rob stop his attack and hop onto the wardrobe beside me.

He stared down at Fellah, who glared and glowered up at us.

'Erk,' said Rob, very seriously, and I have to confess, if I were the monkey, I would have been scared.

Well!

Saved by a ravenlet!

On the one hand, I was a little embarrassed not to have been able to defend myself but, on the other …

Well, it was rather nice, I thought, to have someone on my side.

I gave Rob a friendly little peck on the head.

'*Erk!*' he said, happily.

Good, I thought, he knows who's in charge. Good.

Now this scene in Cudweed's bedroom was all very well, and quite interesting, but what happened next was more interesting.

I'm going to have to think about how I can explain this next bit, so talk among yourselves for a minute and I'll get back to you.

While I do my thinking, you could try counting to eleventy-eight, or check all your toes are still there. When you're done, I'll be ready.

Okay?

Good.

So, having thought about this, I think I can only explain it like this.

First of all, there wasn't a moose in

Cudweed's bedroom.

Then there was.

Then, there wasn't again.

It all happened so fast that I think no one could quite believe it, but I knew what I'd seen, and from the look on everyone else's faces, so did they.

'Did you … ?' began Solstice.

'Was that a … ?' tried Cudweed.

'Erk?' said Rob.

Yes, I thought, a moose appeared in the room, then disappeared again, double quick.

And just in case we had experienced a mini-mass hallucination, there was one undeniable piece of evidence that the moose had been there, and that evidence was smelly and also steaming slightly in a small pile on the carpet.

'Solstice … ?' said Cudweed, nervously.

'Cudweed,' replied Solstice, also nervously.

I knew what they meant.

Even by the weirdly high and highly weird standards of Castle Otherhand, there was only one possible conclusion.

That. Was. Odd.

'Do you think we should go and tell Mother and Father?' Cudweed said.

'Erm,' said Solstice. 'Let me think about that …'

'**Ark!**' I said, which meant, definitely not. The family has enough to worry about without mentioning phantom moose spoiling the carpets of the castle.

Rob agreed with me.

'**Erk,**' he said.

'Well, I don't know,' Solstice said. 'But if it happens again, Cudweed, come and tell me right away?'

Cudweed nodded.

'But where are you going?' he asked, as Solstice headed for the door.

'I'm going to get a dustpan and brush and a plastic bag,' she said, wrinkling her nose at the moose's calling card. 'And then,' she said, looking utterly miserable, 'I'm going to go and start packing my things.'

She went, and Rob and I took one look at Fellah, Cudweed, and the moose's present, and decided that life might be nicer elsewhere.

We flew together down the hallway, and I suddenly thought what a nice thing it was to have some company that could actually fly.

It might even, I thought, be fun. Sometimes.

And that thought made me remember that we probably had just a few days or weeks at most left in the castle.

And that thought made me determined to save everyone. Again.

Everyone. Including me.

'**Ark-rark. Kurk?**' I said to Rob.

'**Erk,**' he said.

Good, I thought. Let's get on with it then.

MAKING MONSTERS!!
Dr. A.N. Ballard
MY LIFE AT THE EDGES OF SCIENCE

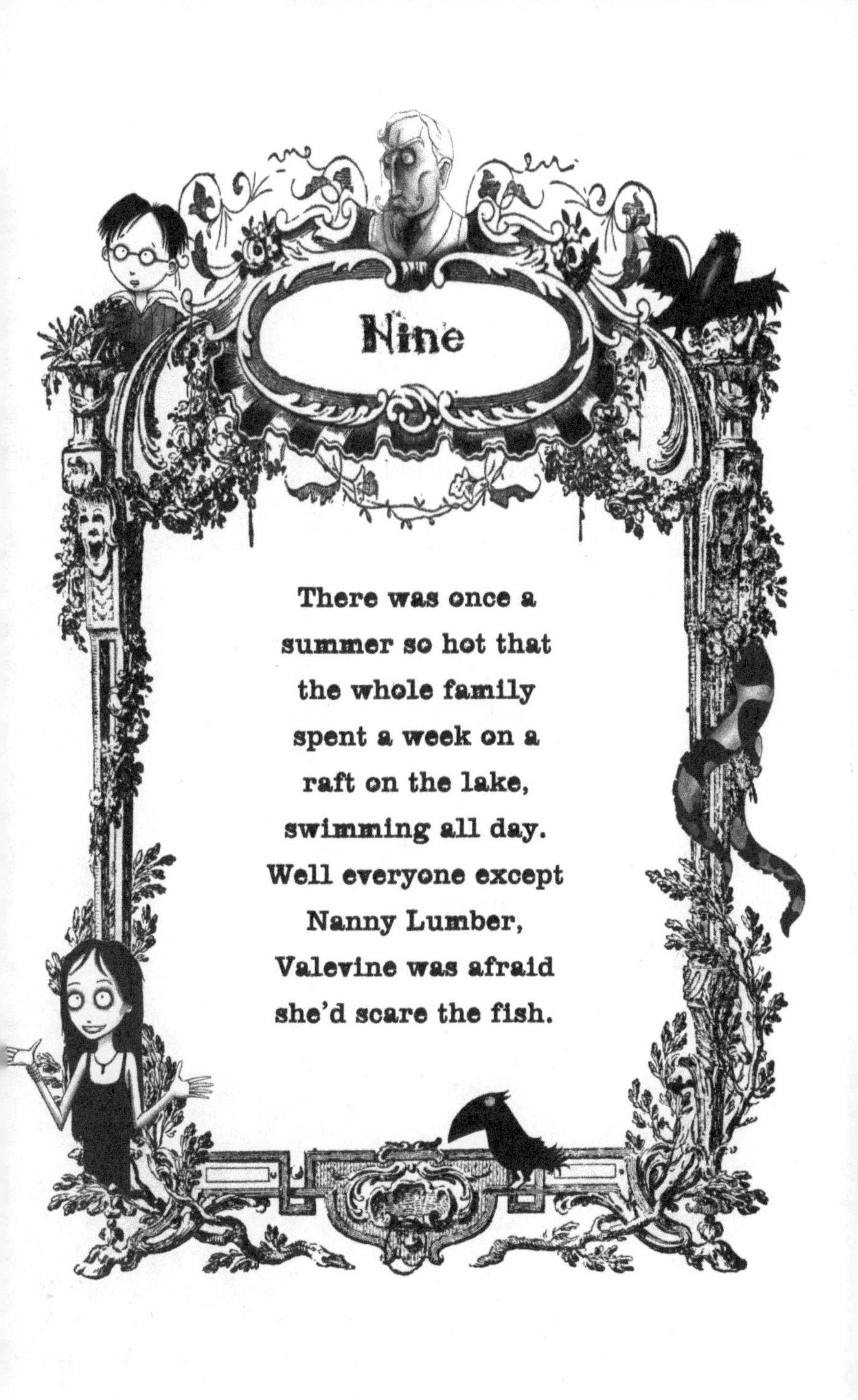

Nine

There was once a summer so hot that the whole family spent a week on a raft on the lake, swimming all day. Well everyone except Nanny Lumber, Valevine was afraid she'd scare the fish.

The only problem was how.

How were we going to find the fabulous lost treasure of Otherhand and save the castle and the lives of everyone in it? How, when hundreds of people had tried, and failed, for hundreds of years?

Rob and I flew to a special secret thinking spot I know between some crazy chimneys on the roof. We had a little discussion.

It went like this.

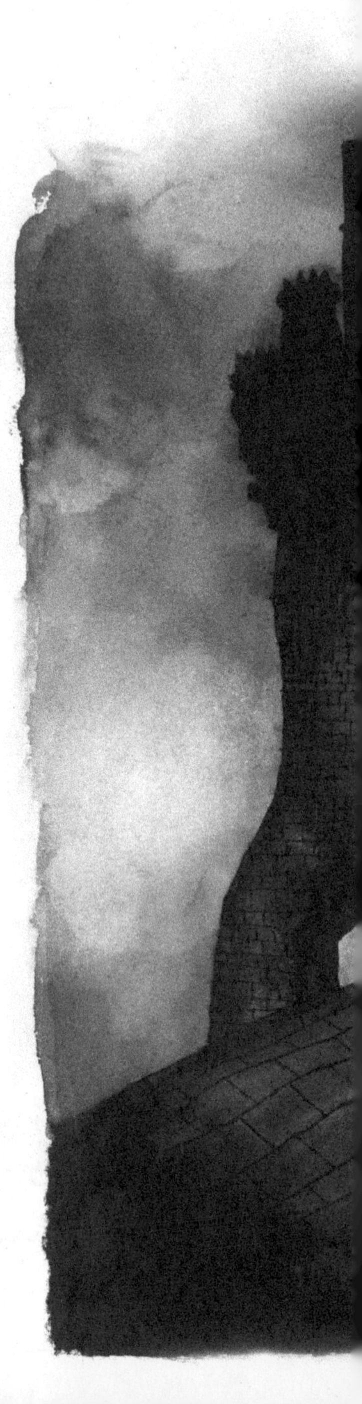

Me: **Ark?**

Rob: **Erk.**

Me: **Ra-ar-kurk. Kurk.**

Rob: **Erk.**

Me: **Kaw! Kaw-kawk, rawk!**

Rob: **Erk?**

Me: **Erk.**

Now, once again, without wasting your time too much, the upshot of all of that was that we didn't have a clue what to do, and couldn't see any way in which we might work out how to know what to do.

The last part of the conversation was me suggesting to Rob that in that case we may as well just sit around and sulk and wait to be carted out of the castle in boxes with the rest of the old junk, and Rob replying that he doesn't 'do' sulking, and that he would prefer to try and keep perky, all the same.

Very odd young fellow, but I suppose youngsters must be allowed to have their own little ways.

So then we were wondering whether to

sulk or be perky. I decided to pull rank and was about to tell Rob that we were going to spend the rest of the day sulking, when I spotted that he'd already tumbled back off the chimney stack and was flying down across the courtyard.

Sighing, and muttering something quite rude in raven speech, I tipped off the roof and followed him.

He was fast, and it was hard to keep up. In a moment he was over the roofs again and heading for the front of the castle, where, it being two o'clock, we saw a gaggle of strangers – the three families come to look at the house.

At the head of this posse was Mr Binkum, waving his hands and pointing at this and that. I don't think he saw us, far above, but

we saw him all right, and did not like what we saw one bit.

He had folders and clipboards and tape measures and everything an estate agent needs to convince even the most reluctant buyer to buy the house he's showing them.

'**Ark! Ark!**' I called to Rob, meaning, well we might not be able to find the treasure but at least we might be able to delay someone buying the castle. If for example, we were able to make them think the castle was full of loud and noisy ravens, or that it was a seriously dangerous place to live, that might just do the trick.

It seemed that Rob agreed.

'**Erk**,' he said, in his usual chirpy fashion.

But how best to start this campaign?

'**Erk**,' said Rob again, full of bright ideas.

So we headed for the Small Hall, to await their arrival.

We were speeding along a corridor, when, passing an open doorway, something caught my eye.

There was a sudden blinding flash of light beyond the doorway, coming from the music room, and then it was gone. I threw on my brakes and circled to see what it might have been, and then stopped so quickly in mid air that Rob nearly flew into the back of me.

Well, my beak nearly bent with surprise.

Not able to believe what I was seeing, I told Rob to fetch Solstice, while I kept an eye on the music room.

When they returned, nothing more had happened, and the room was just as we'd found it.

Upside down.

Yes, upside down. Everything that used to be on the floor was on the ceiling, and vice verse. In fact, that's not a very good explanation because the ceiling itself was where the floor used to be and the floor where the ceiling is supposed to hang out.

'Gasp!' said Solstice. 'What on earth has happened?'

'**Grark!**' I suggested.

Solstice looked at me, and brave but foolish girl that she is, she stepped forward into the room.

There was another flash of light, and then, there she was walking along upside down on the ceiling, or rather, the floor, but the floor was where the ceiling was supposed to be.

She turned and looked at us.

'Why are you all upside down?' she asked, puzzled.

'**Rawk!**' I said, rather stroppily.

Anyone could see that it was her that was the wrong way up.

She strolled about for a bit, and though she was upside down and walking on the 'ceiling', she showed not the slightest fear that she might fall off.

In fact, I noticed that her hair was not dangling down, as it should have been. It was pointing at the floor, her floor, just as if she was not upside down at all.

I think she realised the same thing about the same time, because, looking at us, she picked up a book from the table, and let it drop, and from where we were standing, it fell upwards.

'There,' she said, 'you see. It's you who's upside down.'

Well, not wanting to have a long discussion about it, I flew down the corridor and returned with an apple in my beak, and promptly let it go.

'Gasp!' cried Solstice, 'Your apple fell upwards!'

Or at least, it seemed to have done from where she was standing.

'**Ur-urk!**' I said to Solstice.

'Maybe I should come out of here,' she said, nervously, and headed back for the doorway, whereupon there was another flash of light and there she was, the right way up, with us again.

'I wonder,' she said, gazing back into the room. Then she picked up my apple, and gently tossed it through the open doorway.

The apple began its journey normally enough, starting up, then heading down, but as it crossed the threshold into the room, there was another tiny flash of light, as it curved upwards and landed with a couple of bounces on the 'ceiling'.

'That,' said Solstice very slowly, 'is strange.'

I said nothing, because it seemed there was nothing sensible to say.

'I'm beginning to wonder,' she continued, 'if … No, never mind.'

'Ark?' I asked. What are you wondering? Are you wondering what I'm wondering? Because I'm wondering what you're wondering and if we're both wondering the same thing then that actually might not be so … wonderful.

'Maybe we should go and have a little chat with Mother. Or Father,' she continued, 'Or both. Come on, ravens, let's go and find them.'

And we would have done, but that's when we found out that all the stairs from the first floor to the ground floor had turned into jelly.

Raspberry jelly, in case you're interested.

Ten

There have been
several fires
in the castle's
history. The
biggest one burnt
down an entire
wing, the smallest
singed a couple of
pumpkins and
a mouse.

Solstice wisely decided that it was NOT a good idea to try and descend a staircase made of jelly, especially when there were so many suits of armour with pointy spears waiting at the bottom.

'Besides,' she said. 'Have you noticed how there hasn't been a death in the castle for several weeks?'

'Kaw-awk,' I agreed.

She was right. We were *overdue*. Way overdue. And I didn't want to see our precious teen Goth getting impaled like an aubergine at a vegetarian barbecue.

Given that Minty would about now be shaking hands with Mr Binkum in the Small Hall and welcoming the potential purchasers of Castle Otherhand, that meant that we could only turn for help to one person, Lord Valevine. It was either him, or Nanny Lumber, and nothing on earth would persuade me to enter her private rooms, especially when she was ill.

So Lord Otherhand it would have to be!

We guessed rightly that Valevine would be in his laboratory, working on his automatic packing machine, so we set off for the East Wing.

On the way, however, we were to learn that a simple stroll, or indeed flap, through the castle was a thing of the past.

The first thing we saw was Fellah. As it happens, we barely saw him; he flashed past the end of a long gallery as if a horde of hungry chimpanzees was behind him, which, it turned out, there was. The thought of Fellah being

terrorised by a small army of his close cousins was odd enough, and once again, I almost felt sorry for him, but I would like to draw your attention to the continuing presence of the word 'almost' in this rather long and ungrammatical sentence.

'Gasp!' said Solstice. 'What *is* going on in this castle?'

A short while later as we climbed up through the castle, we passed the nursery. Solstice thought it might be a good idea to check on the twins, as no one probably had for a few days. There they were, quite happy.

Quite happy, for sure, racing miniature

pigs up and down the length of the nursery. I felt sure it was more appropriate to worry about the health and safety of the pigs rather than either Fizz or Buzz.

'Fizz and Buzz!' Solstice said sternly. 'Where did you get those pigs from?'

One of the twins, and it might have been Fizz and it might have been Buzz called back to us, 'one!', by which I think he, or she, meant to show that she, or he, could count.

We left them to it, but the oddities continued.

Passing a closed door on the fifth floor, we heard a roaring noise behind it, and Solstice opened it to find a waterfall the size of a baby Niagara behind the door.

'Erk,' said Rob, and Solstice shut the door quickly behind her.

After that, we couldn't help opening all the doors.

Solstice opened one to find that beyond the room stretched into outer space. The stars and a moon floated into infinity. Just in case there was any doubt, a satellite went past, beeping every three seconds or so, a few lights twinkling on it.

Another opened on a rollercoaster ride heading straight towards us. Solstice slammed the door shut,

expecting the ride to come smashing through it a moment later, but nothing happened.

Cautiously opening another door, we saw a field of sheep. Sheep riding motorbikes. Motorbikes made of hamburgers. Hamburgers made of, I'm glad to say, hamburgers. There the oddness ended, but it seemed the oddness did not end for us, back in the castle.

'Come on,' said Solstice, 'I think we'd better go and see Father as soon as we can. While we still can.'

But that's easier said than done when you're changing size every minute, which is what happened to us next.

As we walked down the hall, I saw that Solstice had become a giant and that Rob and I were midgets. Then, a minute later, our sizes were reversed, and Solstice was so small she could have taken a ride on my back, or even Rob's.

Fortunately, by the end of that corridor, we were all the right size again, leaving us with the small problem of how to cross a wide river of gravy, infested with crocodiles looking for something to make the gravy go further.

Eleven

Once, when Solstice was small, she got lost in the woods. She wasn't frightened. She used the chance to write some scary poems called Slithering Things, Dark and Deadly, and Alone and Lost and Not Happy.

Solstice looked at the crocodiles.

The crocodiles looked at Solstice.

They appeared to be pretty peckish, and were eyeing her up partly because she was bigger than Rob and me, and partly I suspect because she was land-based.

It was clear that young Rob and I would be able to fly over the gravy river and its snapping occupants, where Solstice could not.

'I think maybe we should take another way round,' Solstice said.

'Ark!' I announced. I had turned to find that a second crocodile-infested river had materialised behind us, though, I noted with interest, this one was made of custard.

'Gasp!' gasped Solstice. 'Now what do

we do?'

Make your choice, I thought. Savoury or sweet. Main course or pudding. It's your funeral.

Solstice had other ideas.

'Edgar, Rob, can you distract them? Just for a moment. It's really not so wide. I'm sure I can jump it as long they're not trying to nibble me.'

She pointed at the nearest reptile, who, I have to say, looked as though he wanted to do much more than nibble Solstice.

'Kawk!' I cried.

'Erk,' said Rob, and we hovered and fluttered over the two crocs in the gravy river, while Solstice prepared herself for the jump.

'Rar!' I said, which was me basically saying please get on with it. Rob, being so young and sprightly, was having no trouble dodging the chomping teeth of the crocs, but I was in danger of losing a tail feather or three.

Solstice ran, and jumped, and good for her, made a clean landing on the other side. We quickly joined her – the crocs were looking peeved that their mid-morning snack had just run off.

And run off Solstice did, with raven large and raven small by her side, heading for the East Tower and the laboratory of Lord Valevine Otherhand.

We burst into the lab without knocking to see Lord Otherhand peering into the box we'd seen earlier, and Flinch, for some unknown reason, playing a banjo.

Valevine turned in surprise.

'Solstice, mine of daughter, ah!' he said, and right there and then we should have known that something was up.

Solstice spoke fast, desperate to tell her father all the weird things that we'd seen.

'On going is weird something!' she said. 'Castle the in!'

'What?' barked Valevine.

Solstice tried again.

'Castle the in on going odd something is there.'

Then she added a word that we all understood.

'Gasp!'

'What?' roared Valevine. 'That like talking you are why?'

'Gasp!' exclaimed Solstice again. 'Too you!'

It took me a moment to work out what was going on, but it seemed Solstice had cracked it straight away.

'Backwards out coming is say we sentence every! That is weird how?'

'Girl, what?!' Valevine spluttered.

'Father, yourself to listen!' she explained.

I decided to try it for myself.

'**Awk, kawk, rark,**' I said.

Hah! She was right!

Solstice seemed to be thinking, thinking hard.

'Something try to going I'm.'

A look of fiendish concentration came over her face.

'If … I … talk … backwards … maybe … it … will … come … out … normally.'

She breathed a sigh of relief.

'Hard was that, bother!'

Then she scowled.

'I … mean. Bother, that … was … hard.'

'Girl, about talking you are blazes in what?!'

Now, you're busy people, so I won't detain you, because this conversation went on for some time, with Solstice having to work out everything she wanted to say, backwards, before she said it.

Then she tried something else.

'Wonder I…'

She stepped out of the lab, and spoke normally.

'I wonder if it's only … yes! It only happens in your laboratory, Father!'

'Understand don't still I,' Valevine said.

Eventually, Solstice managed to get her father to step out of the room, and explain what was happening.

'But that's ridiculous!' declared Lord Otherhand.

'I know!' said Solstice, 'but that's not the least of it! There are rivers of crocodiles appearing all over the castle, and you can't get to the first floor because the staircases are all made of jelly!'

'What kind of jelly?' asked Valevine suspiciously.

Solstice's face displayed a mixture of irritation and bemusement.

'Raspberry, I think,' she said.

'I see!' cried Valevine. 'Oh well, can't be helped. Better get on with the packing machine ...'

He turned to go.

'Wait!' called Solstice. 'You can't just ignore this! You must help us! The whole screwy castle is going barmy. Look! There's another example – Flinch is playing the banjo!'

Valevine raised an eyebrow.

'Oh, that?' he said, 'He's playing a banjo because I told him to.'

'Why, Father dear?'

'Because *I* can't. Of course.'

'But neither can he. Clearly.'

Valevine's second eyebrow joined his first one.

'Hmm. Good

point. Okay, I'll come and see what all this fuss is in the castle. Now, where's your mother? And your brother?'

'Thank you, Father,' Solstice said with obvious relief. 'Cudweed's still packing. And Mother was supposed to be meeting Mr Binkum and the new buyers at two in the Small Hall. Maybe we should start there ...?'

'Very well, come on daughter, come Edgar, come ... little Edgar. Let's go and see what's what. What?'

'But Father, it's not safe. The rivers of custard! The staircases of jelly!'

'Hah!' cried Lord Otherhand. 'Mere trifles. Flinch, bring out the abseiling equipment, it's time to get to the ground the fast way!'

So we did, and I hoped for two things.

First, that this latest set of escalating nonsense would soon be sorted out.

And second, that he hadn't meant that joke about trifle, because if he had, it was unbelievably poor, even by his standards.

Vol.XXI

Twelve

Edgar has spent many hours in front of the mirror trying to see if he can smile, but because of his beak, he can't. The best he can do makes it look as if he has wind.

There was no time to be wasted, and yet, I could sense Solstice's reluctance to get into abseiling gear and descend the wall of the East Tower. Solstice is a brave and adventurous girl, but anyone in their right mind would be wary of getting into one of Valevine's contraptions.

'Father … ?' asked Solstice, cautiously. 'Is this your own design?'

'What? These ropes and whatnot? I'm afraid not, Daughter. I bought them off the shelf, as it were. I know you'd prefer to travel in something I'd made myself, but there we are. I haven't got round to climbing gear yet.'

That cheered Solstice up no end.

'Flinch! Find a small basket or something and lower the birds down to the ground, will you, while I get these ropes sorted out.'

'Father,' said Solstice. 'I think Edgar and Rob can probably fly down. That's what they, you know, do.'

Valevine considered this for a moment. 'Yes, I suppose that could work too.'

To show him it could, Rob and I led the way out of the window, one of the highest in the tower, and flapped eagerly outside, waiting for the clumsy people to follow us.

I started to have my doubts about Valevine's abseiling gear, or rather, about his ability to use it.

He pulled it out of a box which had clearly never been opened before, found the instruction booklet, peered at the cover, threw it away, and within moments he looked like a large black spider in a web of spaghetti.

Minutes later, and Flinch was dangling upside down about two hundred metres from the ground.

'Sir?' he called up to Valevine. 'Sir? I think this may not be going according to plan.'

Undaunted, Valevine and Solstice launched themselves after him, and set about untangling him.

That led to all three of them hanging by their ankles a mere hundred metres or so from the ground.

'Ah,' said Valevine.

'Father!' cried Solstice. She sounded worried.

Flinch coughed.

'Sir?'

'What is it, man?' said Lord Otherhand. 'Can't you see I'm busy?'

'Yes, sir, but I think I should tell you I saw something rather peculiar down on the ground.'

'There's something peculiar going on here too,' roared Valevine, 'in case you hadn't noticed! Now be quiet and let me think!'

Rob landed on Flinch's feet. I landed on Solstice's. All four feet were pointing at the sky.

I was tired of flapping.

'**Kerk**,' I said to Rob.

'**Erk**,' he agreed.

I think by that point I had really started to like the young chap.

And then, from somewhere inside the castle came the distant sound of a scream.

'That can't be good,' said Solstice quietly. 'Father! We need to get down from here and find out what's happening! Do something!'

'Ah! I have it!' cried Valevine. 'Gravity! Flinch, pass me your penknife will you?'

Before anyone could stop him, Valevine was sawing at the ropes.

'Father! No! Don't! We'll all be killed!'

'You worry too much,' said Valevine and, moments later, first Flinch, and then Solstice and Lord Otherhand were plummeting towards the ground.

Well, with nothing to perch on, Rob and I hurtled down too and, fortunately for us, we both remembered to starting beating our wings again.

I even tried to grab hold of Solstice, but there was no way I was going to be able to stop her from falling, so fall she did.

The reason that all three were not killed stone dead, and squashed as flat as a disappointed stingray, was due to the sudden appearance of a large fish pond at the base of the tower.

When all three surfaced, covered in pondweed and large amounts of slime, this fact was not lost on them.

'Gasp!' said Solstice. 'Curious!'

'I thought I saw it there,' claimed Valevine.

'Whatever is going on in this place,' Solstice said, 'at least not all of it is dangerous to one's health.'

'Ark!!' I cried. **'Ark!!'**

Because it seemed the three were not the only inhabitants of the fish pond. A large shark fin was cutting towards them through the water.

'Ark!'

'Eeek!' they cried, and scrambled out of the water, leaving a hungry looking shark snapping at their ankles.

Now we hurried to the Small Hall.

'There's no time to waste!' cried Valevine. 'Look!'

He pointed to the roof, which seemed to be turning into cheese. That nice smelly stuff with holes, from Switzerland I think. Great cheese. Not ideal as a roof, it must be said.

'We have got to get to the bottom of this!' cried Valevine, starting to show a genuine desire to live up to his name as lord and master of the castle.

We burst into the Small Hall and found ... no one.

Well, almost no one.

In the centre of the room stood the horrible Mr Binkum, but there was no sign of his buyers, or Minty, for that matter, either.

'Gasp!' Solstice exclaimed. 'Look at the ceiling!'

We all looked, and saw that somehow there was no ceiling, but just a vast swirling massive black hole, with crazy twinkling lights whirling about inside it. Strange shapes and colours oozed and seethed inside the spinning hole.

'What is THAT?' she added.

Valevine stood with his hands on his hips, inspecting the strange thing hovering above our heads where the ceiling should have been.

I decided to sit on the bust of Lord Defreeque, and I noticed Rob had had a similar idea, and perched on a small cannon that stood beside the front door.

Valevine made his announcement.

'That,' he said, 'is a mystical, strange, whirling, space-time vortex thingummy.'

'Ah,' said Solstice. 'I thought it was. Mr Binkum, why are you here all alone? Have you seen anyone else?'

Mr Binkum did not reply. How rude, I thought, but then, as Solstice repeated her question, and got a bit closer, we all noticed that he had been standing very still indeed.

'Mr Binkum ... ? Are you all right?'

He was not.

He was, in fact, a statue of the former estate agent. A stone statue.

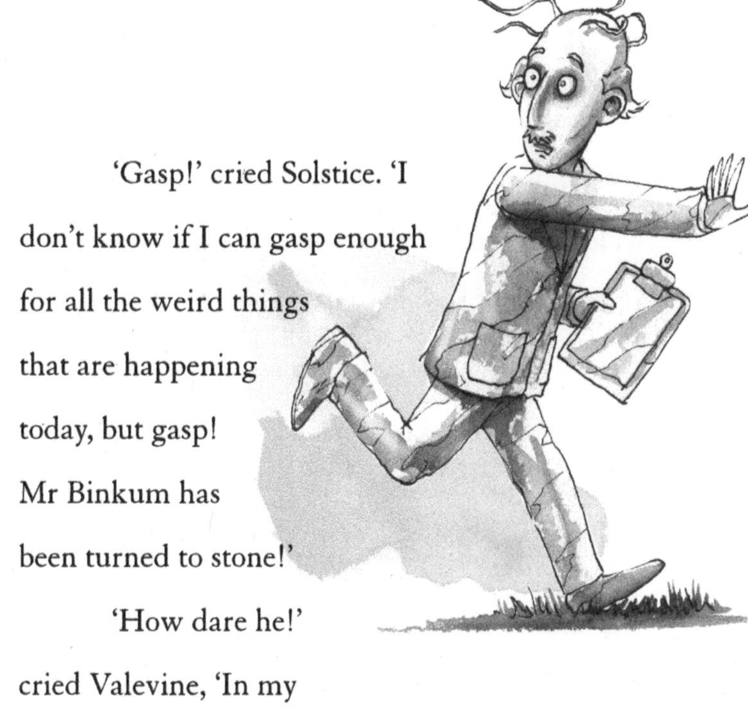

'Gasp!' cried Solstice. 'I don't know if I can gasp enough for all the weird things that are happening today, but gasp! Mr Binkum has been turned to stone!'

'How dare he!' cried Valevine, 'In my castle! Without my permission!'

'Father, I hardly think that's the point! The point is, what are we going to do? Something did this to him, something that's probably on the loose in the castle right now!'

Flinch coughed, as if he wanted to speak, but no one listened to him.

'You're right, daughter of mine!' declared Valevine. 'And furthermore, whatever can have unleashed all this nonsense upon us? What!?'

Solstice looked sheepish.

'Ah,' she said, 'Well, I think that might be my fault.'

And she told her father about the spell she and Cudweed had made, at the end of which, Valevine looked very stern indeed.

'Let this be a lesson to you,' he growled, 'not to mess with your mother's spell books. Something serious might have happened!'

Solstice looked at Mr B.

'I think it has,' she said unhappily.

'Very well,' said Valevine. 'There's only one hope for us. We need your mother's skills.

If you can show her the spell, she can probably undo it.'

Yes, I thought, as long as we're not all turned to stone, or indeed cheese, first.

SISTERS OF
DOOM!
our memoir
H. and G. PELLING

Thirteen

A pair of eagles once decided to set up home in the castle, and made a nest on top of the East Tower. Edgar was not impressed, and within a week he had pecked them into leaving.

Valevine decided it was time to make one of his famous rallying speeches, to rouse us all into action. Unfortunately for him, he had an audience of only five, two of whom were bored birds, and one of whom was an estate agent made of stone.

Valevine waved his arms about for a bit, trying to sound impressive, but to be honest he was upstaged by the swirling space-time vortex thingummy.

'So!' he finished. 'It all comes down to this. Are we to sit idly by while our entire world falls about our ears? Or shall we fight? Fight for what is ours! Well, I tell you, I know what I'm going to do! And I think you do too!'

Solstice, bless her, gave her father a round of applause, but then spoilt it rather by adding, 'maybe we should get on with it? Now?'

'Ahem,' said Valevine, 'Very well. Now, the thing is this. The castle is becoming wilder and weirder. We need to find Minty and we need to find the spell book that you used. And then we need to get the two of them together and see what they can do, right? Right.'

'And,' said Solstice. 'We ought to see that everyone is okay. Cudweed. The twins

and Grandma Slivinkov. Even
Nanny Lumber. And Fellah.'

Well, I agreed with Solstice on the first four. The last two could be turned into jellyfish for all I cared.

'Quite right, quite right!' exclaimed Valevine. 'And there may be a gang of lost house buyers around here somewhere too. The question is this, do we split up, or join forces? Safety in numbers, and all that?'

'I think,' said Solstice, 'we should split up. Given the rate at which the castle is turning odd, we need to work fast.'

'Quite so!' said Valevine. 'Flinch! You are to find and rescue Grandma, Cook and Nanny Lumber! Solstice! You are to find your brother and the twins! Edgar and little Edgar, you are to find the spell book! I will find your mother. We will meet back here as soon as possible!'

Solstice looked at the mysterious space-time vortex thingummy.

'Maybe,' she said, 'Maybe we should meet somewhere else? Just in case that thing is as dangerous as it looks.'

'Hmm,' said Valevine. 'A fair point! Maybe ...'

But just as he said this, the mystical strange space-time vortex thingummy disappeared.

A second later, we heard another distant scream, and then the sound of rocks rattling on the roof. At least, that's what it sounded like.

'Right, everyone. No time to waste, back

here as soon as possible. Got it? Edgar and little Edgar. If you find the book quickly, you can then act as communication between Solstice, Flinch and I. Solstice, take paper, pencil and string with you. We will do the same. Right! Now go!'

'Awk, awk, kark!'

I announced.

Valevine didn't understand me, but that's nothing new.

'Good bird!' he said, when what I'd actually said was that in the first place I didn't think we'd be able to carry the spell book between us, and secondly, even if we could, spending my last hours in the castle acting as a carrier pigeon was deeply degrading.

Solstice had understood however, for

she held up her arm, and when I flapped down from the bust of Defreeque, she tickled me under the chin.

'Oh Edgar,' she cooed. 'Are you going to be a big brave bird for us again, and save the day? I know you can. And if you do, I'll make sure there are *thousands* of dried mice for you to eat, and some for Rob too.'

Well, soft old bird that I am, that was enough to seal the deal.

'**Awk**,' I said, gently.

Just when it seemed that things couldn't get any worse, they did.

The front door swung open, and three men in horribly neat grey suits arrived.

'We're from the bank,' their leader

announced. 'And, though this is technical banking speak that you may not understand, we're totally cheesed off. We've had it. We want our money back, and we're fed up waiting for you to sell this old wreck of a house. We have a large corporation lined up, ready and waiting with the cash. If you don't give us our money by the end of the day, we're going to sell your castle to them. They have plans to turn it into a luxury hotel and health spa. Either that or a lunatic asylum for the dangerously insane.'

Well, I thought. No change there then.

With that, the three bankers slammed the

door behind them, and left us to our doom.

Only a few hours left to get rid of a mystical space-time vortex thingummy, save everyone from whatever was roaming the castle, and find a squillion or two in cash.

Well, to a raven of my abilities, I thought, that *almost* presents a challenge worth getting out of bed for.

I winked at Solstice.

'Edgar, are you feeling all right?' she asked. 'Is there something wrong with your eye?'

Blast the girl. I was trying to look noble and heroic.

With that, Rob and I sped from the Small

Hall as if someone had announced free squashed squirrels two valleys away.

Fourteen

The castle was once infested by rats. Then, one day, they were all gone. Shortly afterwards, everyone began asking Cook why her stew tasted different. She didn't answer.

Rob and I whizzed through the castle and, as we did, I once again had the most peculiar feeling that it was nice to have company, by which I mean, company with feathers.

People are all very well, but you know, they do have funny habits and strange opinions. Not like ravens. Ravens are simple creatures really, when you get to know them. Somewhere nice to sulk and a couple of dried mice, and you've pretty much guaranteed yourself a happy bird.

As we flew, I thought I would take the chance to find out more about Rob. Where, for example, had he come from?

I asked him.

'Krark?' I said, as we rounded a corner and headed for Minty's library.

'Erk,' said Rob.

Well, that explained one or two things, but quite frankly it asked as many questions and it answered. I decided to press him a little further.

'Kaw-urk?'

'Erk, erk,' said Rob.

Well, there you are then, mystery solved!

Fancy that, though, eh? It's a small world, as they say, though I wouldn't want to paint it.

We were making good progress on our mission, and the only weird things we'd seen were three striped pigs wandering in the Long Gallery, looking lost, and Cook, floating like a cloud down the centre of the stairwell. Interestingly she was still trying to mix cake batter.

So we were confident of making a quick

and easy raid on Minty's library, which lies on the sixth floor.

We came into the corridor, saw the door at the far end, and hurtled down. Just as we reached the door there was an odd popping noise, and we found ourselves back at the beginning of the corridor.

'Errrrk?' said Rob.

Gosh, his vocabulary was getting bigger every minute.

'Rak!' I said, and we tried again.

The same thing happened. Just as we got to the door, there was the same sucking popping noise, and I noted an odd lurch in one's feathery belly, and suddenly we were back where we started.

No doubt this was the work of the space-time vortex whatsit, but we weren't going to be defeated so easily.

As it turned out, we were defeated after three more attempts, by which time we both stood panting on the floor, glaring at the corridor, and the door at the end of it.

I had an idea.

My knowledge of the castle is second to none. It would mean a bit of careful flying, but I knew we could do it.

I asked Rob how he felt about flying through chimneys in pitch blackness.

'Erk!' he said, and I remembered that when I was his age, I too found that sort of thing exciting.

So we set off into the outside world,

guessed which chimney pot we needed, accurately as it turned out, and a few twists and turns later, we exploded into Minty's library in a cloud of soot. We were unscathed and well, even if we were a little dirty from the soot, but that's the great advantage of wearing black all the time – no one knows if you could actually do with a bath.

Two further problems awaited us.

First, as we looked at Minty's collection of spell books, was the problem of knowing which one Cudweed and Solstice had borrowed.

That was soon solved, as the smell of orange juice, being particularly unpleasant to a raven's beak, was easy to detect on one of the books.

Second, and a much greater problem, was the question of how we were going to get the thing out of the room, and how we were going to carry it. The book was much heavier than I'd remembered, the library door turned out to be locked, and the chimney we'd flown through was narrow in places.

Now, it was Rob's turn to have an idea.

'**Er-erk**,' he pointed out.

Of course! We only needed the spell from the book that Solstice and Cudweed had messed around with. And that was obvious to spot because it was the one smeared with croissant crumbs.

I flipped the book open and Rob tore out the section of pages that contained our spell.

With a few deft flicks of the beak, we'd rolled it into a tube small enough for me to carry.

Up and out into the daylight, and then wheeling around, we were dashing back groundwards, for the Small Hall.

And then we saw it.

Between the rows of trees in the orchard, and for a brief second, we saw The Thing! It had at least five tentacles, possibly wings, one head, maybe more, was orange and green, and

had countless legs. As soon as we saw it, it was gone.

Then there was a scream, suddenly cut short.

We dropped to the spot in two moments, but The Thing had gone. All we found was one of the buyers of the castle. Turned, it has to be said, to stone.

'**Awwwwk!**' I cried to Rob.

Now we knew our enemy.

Some strange alien monster, which had no doubt come through the vortex whatsit.

'**Erk**,' Rob said, with quiet determination.

Quite right.

Erk, indeed.

Fifteen

When Cudweed and
Solstice were small,
they believed there
were fairies living
on the lilypads by
the pond, and would
leave treats for them
to eat every evening.

Of course, we were the first back at the Small Hall, and left our spell pages on a side table by the front door. We were just turning to go when Flinch arrived with Grandma Slivinkov.

'Heh,' she said to no one in particular. 'Valevine's man says we have to evacuate the castle! Heh!'

Flinch raised an eyebrow.

'Be so good, your Ladyship,' he said, 'as to wait here while I find Nanny Slumber, and Cook.'

Good luck with both of those things, I thought. One's mad and dangerous at the best of times. The other is floating around somewhere in the North Wing with a large mixing bowl.

And by the time you do get back, Grandma S. is almost certain to have wandered off. Probably somewhere life-threatening.

So good luck. With that.

Rob and I decided to see if we could help.

The most important thing was get Minty and that spell together.

Now, if you've been paying any kind of attention at all over the last couple of years, you will know that the castle is a big place.

Huge, in fact. And therefore, trying to find anyone in anything like a hurry is normally a matter of being extremely lucky.

What we needed was a short cut, and so we made a few fly-overs of the castle, from north to south, gliding as silently as we could, listening for sounds of trouble.

It didn't take long to hear screams coming from the High Terrace and, zooming down, we found Solstice, Cudweed, Fellah and the twins cowering behind a snow fort.

Funny weather for early summer, you might think, and so did I, but not as funny as seeing three large polar bears heading towards the children, though it was Fellah who was the one doing all the screaming.

Solstice had the others well organised.

Fizz and Buzz were making as many snowballs as their little paws could manage, and Cudweed and Solstice were keeping up a frenzied attack on the polar bears.

It seemed enough to keep them at bay, but as soon as Solstice saw us overhead, she wailed.

'Help! Edgar! We're running out of snow!'

It was true, I could see that the twins were scraping up bits of slush now, and Cudweed and Solstice were throwing fewer and fewer snowballs.

The bears, sensing this, were getting closer. One stood on its back legs, roared, and rubbed its tummy.

I got the picture. Hungry bear.

'Futhork!' I cried.

I looked around to see if there were any suitable weapons standing nearby. There weren't.

What there was, however, was the door to the Red Room, not too far away. If we could distract the bears for long enough, the children (and the monkey, sadly) might be able to make a dash for it, and bolt the door behind them.

'**Kurk**,' I said to Rob. '**Ka-kawk!**'

Well, it seemed he'd been thinking what I'd been thinking, so we began an attack on the back of the bears heads.

Futhork!

They were fast for such big creatures. I nearly got swiped by a massive paw, and that would certainly have been the end of poor old Edgar, but as it was, we managed to irritate the bears just enough to make them forget about the others.

As soon as they'd sprinted for the Red Room, however, we stopped our attack and headed for the safety of the skies.

It was then that the alien space thing appeared on the terrace, right behind the bears, who turned, ready for a fight.

Poor things!

They didn't stand a chance. One moment, there were three massive snarling polar bears, the next, there were three nice stone statues on the High Terrace.

'Gasp!' cried Solstice as we joined them in the Red Room. 'Did you see that? We're in big trouble! Big, big trouble!'

'**Ark!**' I agreed.

'Edgar!' she went on, 'Do you know where Father is? Or Mother?'

'**Urk,**' I said, unhappily.

'Well,' said Solstice. 'We have to find them.'

Tell me something I don't know, I thought, but I didn't say it, because it probably wouldn't have helped.

I thought instead that they could do with something inspiring and optimistic.

'Rork!'

'Rork, indeed,' agreed Solstice. 'Did you find the spell at least?'

'Ark!'

'Good birds!' Solstice said. 'Well, maybe we should just stick to Father's plan? Make our way back to the Small Hall and hope he's found Mother and that they are already working on reversing that spell.'

That all sounded like the toppest of top plans, but little did we know what an epic journey we would have to make to get back to the Small Hall from the Red Room.

A journey I hoped never to see the like of again.

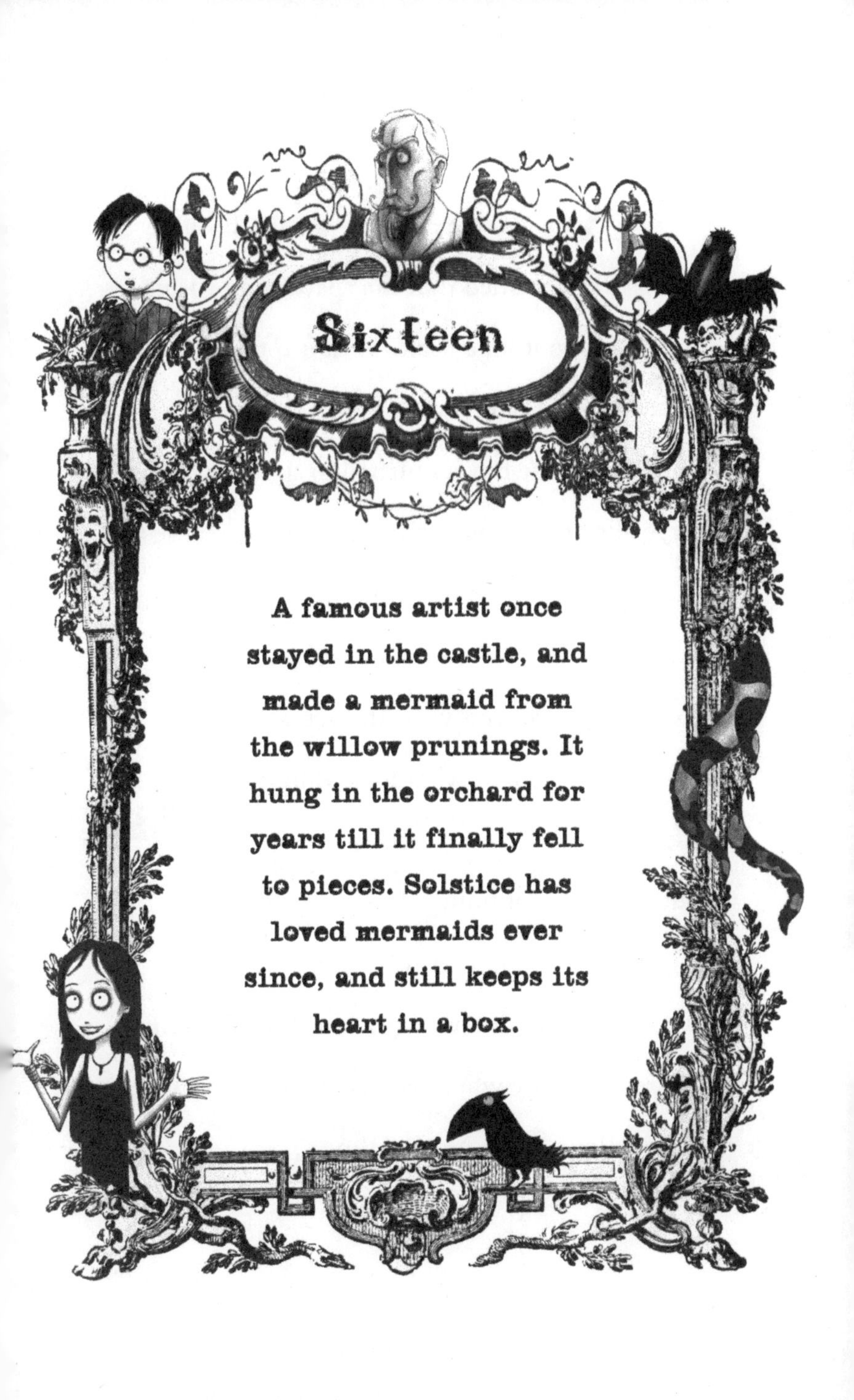

Sixteen

A famous artist once stayed in the castle, and made a mermaid from the willow prunings. It hung in the orchard for years till it finally fell to pieces. Solstice has loved mermaids ever since, and still keeps its heart in a box.

As we made our way warily through the castle, it seemed that the space-time vortex thingy had outdone itself. Most impressive.

So not only did we find a few more potential house buyers turned to stone by the large alien space monster thing, we also realised that the polar bears might not have been as hungry as they were pretending, judging by some of the *leftovers* we came across. I thought I spotted what looked like the remains of James's boots, but not much of him.

We spied other fearsome creatures as we crept along the passages, but things began to get really sticky when we made it down to the fourth floor of the North Wing.

Literally, because the floors there were coated with treacle. That wouldn't have been so bad, were it not for the infestation of ants soon afterwards, outside the music room, which was, it appeared, still upside down. Luckily for us, we bumped into a herd of rather cute anteaters on the next landing, and we were soon free of the little biting fellows, which was a shame for Rob and me, because ants make a very nutritious snack.

For about five minutes we saw or heard nothing unusual, but as we sneaked onto the gallery above the Small Hall, we realised that we were all feeling very out of sorts indeed.

I looked at Solstice. She was about eleven feet tall, but only four inches wide. She was bending and wobbling around like a rubber hose, and then I realised we all were. It was the space-time vortex thingy again, doing its tricky stuff.

'Gasp!' Solstice said, or rather I think she tried to, but her voice had gone all weird, and when I tried to squawk, so had mine. It was as if we were speaking another language. A language made of soup,

that's the only way I can describe it.

We kept on wibbling and wobbling along, however, and, in the end, it proved quite handy: since the stairs were still made of raspberry jelly, we were able to use Cudweed as a rope to lower everyone down to the Small Hall, where the stretchy business wore off.

There, we found Valevine and Minty.

No sign of Flinch and the others yet, and Grandma S. had indeed wandered off somewhere.

'Gasp!' declared Solstice, properly now. 'This is all getting very silly indeed.'

'We were nearly eaten by polar bears!' Cudweed told his mother happily. 'And nibbled by ants and licked clean by anteaters. It was fun! Fellah got really sticky in the treacle though.'

Cudweed seemed unusually brave about everything and it made me wonder if he'd gone slightly mad.

'Never mind the anteaters,' Minty said. 'And no one likes a sticky monkey. You of all people should know that by now.'

'Quite so!' Valevine said, adding darkly.

'Our own path here was not without incident. But here we are! Now, Edgar my boy, do you have that spell book? I've explained everything to Lady Otherhand. She just needs to see which spell it was you mucked about with ...'

Rob nipped over to the table and returned with the pages from the spell book.

'It was the one to locate your cows,' Solstice explained. 'And Mother, I really am very, very sorry about all this. I was just trying to find the fabulous lost treasure and everything, so we wouldn't have to sell the castle and move.'

'I understand dear,' said Minty, which was generous of her. I'm not sure I was feeling so generous, even though I am rather fond of Solstice. This time I think she had possibly gone too far. Too, too far.

Minty was studying the pages, and then began to frown.

'Which spell did you say you used, dears?'

Solstice pointed.

'That one, the one about cows. It goes over onto the next page. See?'

Minty turned the pages over.

'Do you mean these two pages? The ones stuck together with what seems to be orange juice and jam?'

Solstice went a funny colour of white.

'Oh dear,' she said, in a very small voice.

'So, just to be clear, you read the start of this spell here,

and the end of … this one here?'

She turned the pages, and then tried to pull them apart.

'And we changed it all a bit too,' Cudweed said brightly. 'Because it was about cows, and we didn't want cows, we wanted cash.'

I don't think the poor boy had grasped exactly what had happened, or what can happen when you mix two spells together.

'I was reading it out,' he went on, 'And Solstice did the actions and so on.'

'And were you, by any chance, spilling your orange juice on the book at the same time?'

Cudweed suddenly looked less happy.

'It's possible,' he said. 'A bit.'

Minty sighed.

'Oh, my dears, what have you done? This is going to be very tricky to reverse. Very tricky indeed ...'

A deathly hush fell on the Hall, and I prayed that Minty would be able to do it, and do it soon, because at that very moment, a squad of Roman legionaries began to march up and down on the lawn outside, looking very much as if they had plans to invade.

Seventeen

Solstice and Cudweed once had riding lessons. They didn't go again: Cudweed said the bouncing hurt too much and Solstice said it was too energetic for her image.

There are moments in every raven's life when he takes a little time out to stop and consider things deeply.

This wasn't one of them.

There was no thinking to be done. In fact, the only thing to do was to flap about in a panic and a fuss while Minty did her stuff.

It took a while.

First, she tried to insist that we left the Hall, but when everyone said they were too scared to, she gave in.

'You may stay here, but only on the strict condition that no one makes a sound.'

Well, with Fellah in the room, the silence didn't really even get started, so it was a very grumpy Minty who set about undoing whatever it was that Solstice and Cudweed had done.

She muttered and hummed and humphed and tsked and all sorts of other thinking noises, but she didn't actually seem to be doing very much.

Soon, everyone was bored. I took the chance to tell Rob a bit about the castle, and since we were in the Small Hall, I explained its finer features, in particular, the bust of Lord Defreeque. Why? Well, because don't let it be

said I am not a generous bird. I realised that Rob would need a few spots round the castle to use as sulking spots, assuming, that is, that someone found the cash to buy the castle within the next few hours, and that, sooner or later, Rob would come round to my way of thinking, and sulking.

And I felt it only fair that he have some of the same spots as me, in which to practise his art of sulking, but, and I think this is a pretty important point, I felt that the bust of Lord Defreeque should be reserved for my private and unique use, as head raven in the castle.

So I was just explaining all this to him, and bless him, he seemed perfectly happy with the whole arrangement.

'**Erk?**' was the only thing he queried.

'**Awk!**' I assured him.

'**Erk**,' he agreed.

It was about this time that Cudweed, who was gazing out of the window, noticed something else.

'Mother,' he said. 'Father. Everyone. I don't think we need to worry about the Romans any more.'

'That's good, dear,' said Minty over her shoulder, not really listening.

'Yes, well, no,' Cudweed said thoughtfully. 'Not really. You see they've just been wiped out by a flock of … oh … you know, what do you call them … ?'

'What do you call what?' asked Solstice, wandering over to join her brother.

'You know. Those huge lizard things. The ones that were made extinct millions of years ago. Big teeth.'

'You mean, dinosaurs?' cried Solstice.

'Yes! That's them. Dinosaurs! A flock of dinosaurs!'

I doubted that 'flock' was the right word, but it seemed unhelpful to pass comment at that moment.

I did what I thought was right, instead.

 **'Futhork!'** I screeched, and then Minty did have to come over and have a look.

'I think,' she said, 'I might try and do a little different bit of magic first, before I reverse that spell ...'

'What's that, dear?' asked Valevine.

'Well,' Minty said, 'I think I can remember how to cast a protection spell on a room. I think I had better cast one on the Hall here, now. Just so as the dinosaurs don't get us.'

Valevine was delighted.

'Or anything else for that matter! Great idea!'

Solstice had an objection.

'But Mother, if you cast that spell, does that mean that Flinch won't be able to get back in either, with Cook and Nanny Lumber?'

'I'm afraid so, dear.'

'But Grandma S. is missing too! What about her?'

'Well, I think that they may have to take their chances …'

'You can't be serious!' cried Solstice.

I won't go into too many details over what happened next, but let's just say there was a bit of a discussion and leave it at that.

The 'discussion' ended when Flinch arrived in a great hurry, with Cook, Spatchcock, Pete – still clutching his notebook full of sketches – and even Grandma S. in tow.

'Well done, man!' cried Valevine.

'Nanny Lumber?' asked Minty.

'Did you find her?'

Flinch shook his head.

Everyone looked at everyone else. I think everyone was pretty much thinking the same thing as I was: that is to say, I felt more worried for the space alien beast than for Nanny.

Cudweed squealed a little.

'I say, those dinosaurs are *really* big. I think their teeth are longer than I am tall!'

Valevine whispered to his wife.

'Time for that spell, eh, wife?'

'Yes, husband,' said Minty, and a few seconds later, we were all safe inside a magically protected Small Hall – nothing could come in or out.

Cudweed was still staring out of the window.

'Father,' he said, 'Do you think it's okay if the dinosaurs eat the castle?'

'Whaaat?' roared Valevine. He stormed over to Cudweed, as did we all, and watched with horror as two large beasts with road drills for teeth began

chewing lumps out of the old place. 'Any more of this, and there won't be a castle worth saving.'

'Oh look!' cried Solstice. 'More polar bears! They look rather nice in pink, don't they?'

Valevine looked long and hard at the chaotic scenes developing outside the window, then he turned back to Minty.

'Come on, now, Lady Otherhand. I know you can do it. But please do it soon before the mystical weird strange space-time vortex thin-gummyjig creates any more stuff that's going to leave us without a home. A home that, by the way, we don't even own any more.'

Minty got a bit cross then.

'You think I don't know that?' she said, her voice a bit wobbly. 'I never was much good as a witch, and I'm really out of my depth here.'

'You managed to do the protection spell,' said Solstice encouragingly. 'That was great. Only maybe you could try and get rid of the vortex, because at the moment it's just appeared on the front lawns and there are flamingos coming out of it.'

'That sounds quite nice,' said Valevine.

'Flamingos with lasers,' Solstice added.

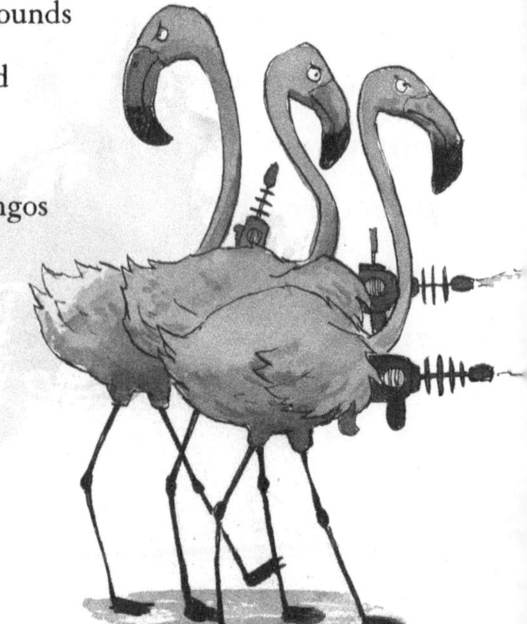

'Right!' cried Minty. 'That's it! I don't really know what I'm doing but ... well, here goes!'

She waved her arms, muttered some really weird words in a really weird voice, waved her arms about some more, and suddenly, there was a loud sucking and whistling sound from outside.

'It vanished!' cried Solstice from the window. 'The vortex just vanished! Oh, Mother! You did it! How clever you are! How clever!'

Everyone cheered.

'There's just one thing,' Solstice added.

'Which is ... ?' asked Cudweed, nervously.

'Well,' she said. 'It looks like the vortex thingy has gone. But it seems as if everything it made is still here. Including the lethal flamingos.

They've just incinerated a pterodactyl.'

And though it's not often you get to say a sentence like that, Solstice didn't seem very happy about it, at all.

Well, it seemed there were just two issues left now. A castle full of weird and frequently dangerous things.

And three nasty bank managers.

I didn't know which was worse.

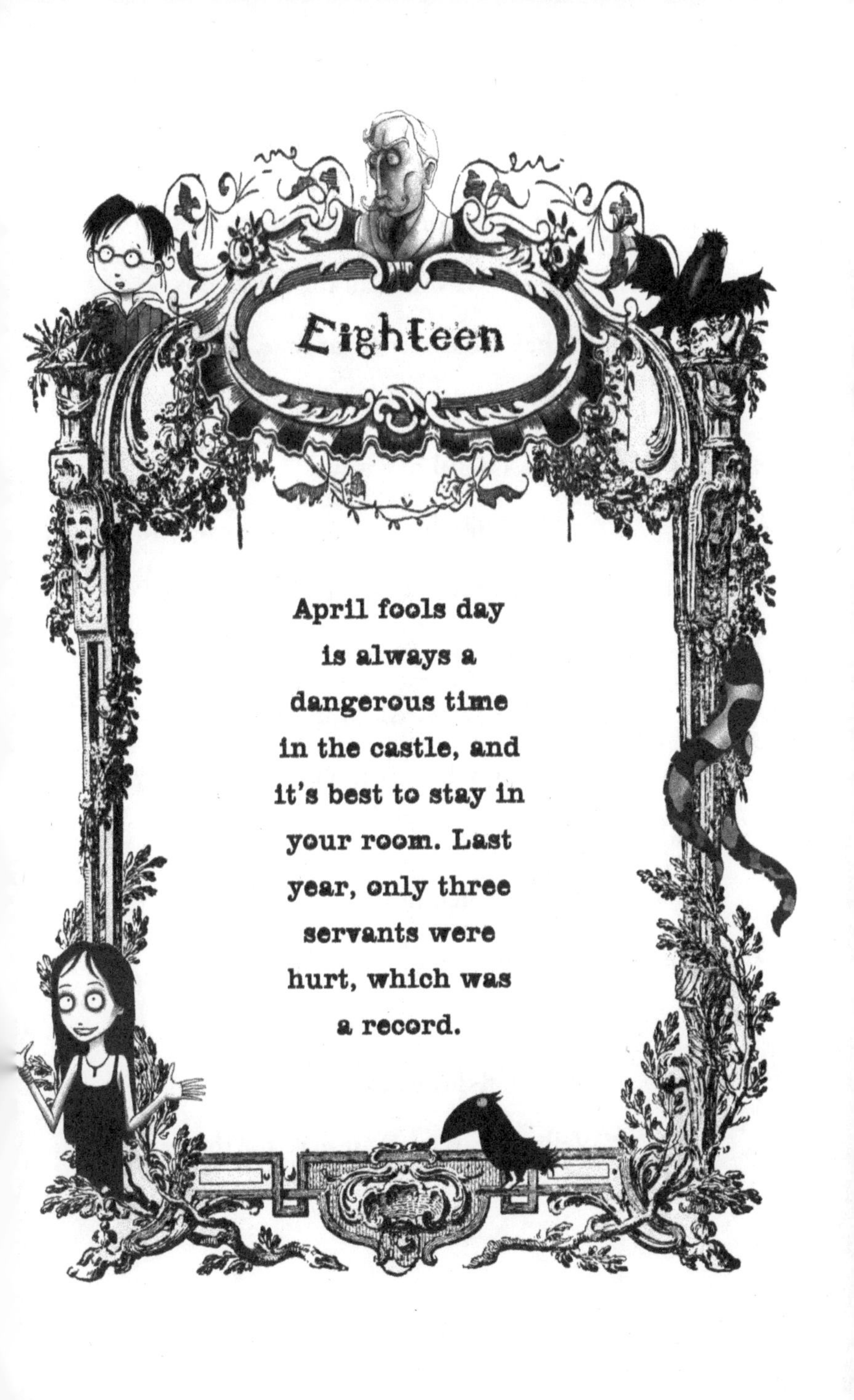

Eighteen

April fools day is always a dangerous time in the castle, and it's best to stay in your room. Last year, only three servants were hurt, which was a record.

That day ended like no other day in Otherhand history. Not in all the hundreds of years since they took over from the Defreeques had the castle seen such weird times.

What a fateful day it was!

And how my beak trembles to even think about the momentous moments that mounted monstrously.

There we were. All of us safe, well all of us except Nanny Lumber, but she was fairly indestructible, wherever she was.

Safe, but stuck in the Small Hall, and with the bank managers due to reappear at any moment, to claim the castle as theirs.

Minty stated the obvious.

'Well, we can't just sit here for the rest of

our lives, can we?'

'Quite so,' agreed Valevine. 'Quite so.'

'So what are we going to do?' his wife asked.

Valevine thought about this for a good minute two.

'I have no idea,' he stated eventually. 'Absolutely none! Isn't that remarkable?'

He seemed quite happy with that conclusion, but no one else was.

'Father!' cried Solstice. 'We must do something!'

'Quite so! Quite, so,' agreed her father, 'But the minute any one of us sets foot outside the hall, it could very easily lead to that space alien turning that person to stone. And that's to say nothing of the other horrors lurking on the lawn … The, er, pink birds with laser beams, for one thing. The, er, dinosaurs, for another.'

'Well,' cried Cudweed, checking on the scene out front. 'Actually, we may not have to worry about them after all.'

'How so?' Valevine asked.

'Because the space alien is there right now. Turning everything to stone. We're going to have some awfully odd statues by the driveway when he's done.'

'Well, that's one less thing to worry about,' sighed Minty, 'But what are we going to do about *him*?'

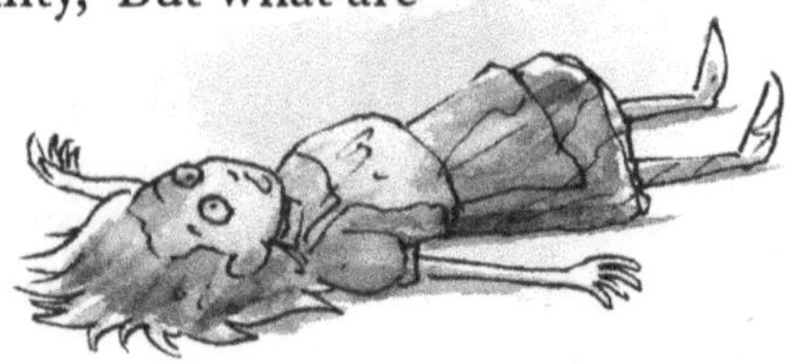

'I have an idea,' Solstice said, brightly. 'But it will need some high explosives, some precision timing, and a very brave raven. Or two.'

As you can imagine, I didn't like the sound of that at all. Valevine, however, was all ears.

'Well,' explained Solstice, 'it goes like this. You see the cannon that Rob is sitting on? As far as I am aware, they should still work, but

we'll need to load them with gunpowder and a cannonball or two. And maybe whatever else sharp and deadly we can find. I suggest we drag them over here, point them at the door, and then, when the alien space monster comes through the door, we let him have it. Right between the eyes. All fifteen of them.'

'Interesting plan,' said Valevine. 'Two small questions. First, where are we going to get the gunpowder from? And second, why is the alien space monster going to saunter through our front door?'

'Aha!' Solstice said. 'You have lots of gunpowder in your laboratory, I'm sure. So Rob is going to fly up there and bring back as much as he can. And Edgar's going to act as bait to lure the beast to the front door, and, just as he gets here, Mother will drop the protection spell, he'll come in, and then… whammo!'

'Ark!' I said, loudly. **'Ark, rark, kawk. Futhork, kark, rakk, ark, ark, futhork! Futhork!'**

Solstice picked a fine time to misunderstand me.

'There! You see, Edgar thinks it's a great plan!'

'FUTHORK!' I squawked, as loudly as I could, but everyone thought I was even more keen to fly to my doom than before.

Only Rob understood.

'Erk!' he said.

But then he added something else.

'Erk.'

And when put like that, what choice did we have but to go along with Solstice's plan? None at all.

So be it.

I would either save everyone, or die nobly and heroically in the process. And while that sounds all very good on paper, I felt that I would much rather sit by the fire with a dried mouse and nothing much to do.

Nineteen

No one knows
how old Edgar is
exactly, even he
doesn't. He's pretty
ancient but, despite
that, he's pretty
sure he'll be going
strong for a while
to come.

Not only did I have to act as bait to lure the beasty to the front door, I also had to keep him distracted and away from Rob while my new young friend made several trips to Valevine's lab.

My wings were aching even before he got back the first time, and as I danced and flapped just out of reach of the snapping chomping alien space beast and his horrible stone-dealing tentacles, I saw Rob patiently collect several sugar bags' worth of gunpowder from the East Tower.

Meanwhile, Solstice and the others had been moving the two small cannons and lining them up with the doorway. It was point-blank range, and all we had to do was get the monster to cooperate and follow me through the door.

That would be easy. Having petrified every other living object outside the castle, I was now his only plaything.

One touch from any of those many tentacles and, I knew, I would drop to the ground, a raven of stone, ready to be sold as a garden ornament for someone's bird bath, albeit a rather sulky-looking one.

Hah! That was not a way I wanted to go, so I flew and dipped and swooped and barrelled my way around the skies, until finally I saw the signal from the window – Cudweed waving like a lunatic.

They were ready!

And not a moment too soon, for my wings hurt like never before.

The beast roared at me from one or two of its mouths as I sped towards the front entrance to the castle.

As I neared, I saw Cudweed waving again frantically, this time to Solstice, to open the doors. Sure enough, as I was but a tentacle's length away, the doors swung open and I zoomed into the safe air of the Small Hall. I landed on the bust of Lord Defreeque, to watch the demise of the monster.

'Now!' screamed, well, everyone.

Blast Valevine!

It was point-blank range, the beast was a sitting duck, and he missed!

'Noooo!' screamed, well, everyone.

'Use the other one! Use the other one!'

That was Solstice. They had prepared both the small cannons by the front door, and so we had one chance left.

'Quickly. Swing it round!'

That was Valevine.

The monster, still enraged, was standing underneath the bust, trying to leap and grab me.

'Now!' wailed, yes, again, everyone, and this time, Valevine did not miss.

Whatever they had loaded into the cannon, it was terrifying. There was an almightily loud bang, and I shot towards the ceiling like a jack-in-a-box.

Just as well, for a cannonball, a couple of heavy rocks, a hundred or so forks, some kitchen knives and various curious ornaments tore into the beast at very high speed.

The thing didn't stand a chance.

One minute there was a truly scary beast rollicking around in the Hall, the next, there was a big pile of goo.

Fellah went over to give it a lick.

Even I wouldn't do that, but no one was paying attention. Everyone was cheering and shouting, and yelling and jumping for joy, that the monster was over.

But not me.

Not me, and just in case you think I was having a quick sulk, let me explain. You see, I had spotted something.

Something rather interesting, something rather important.

For where the cannonball and all its lethal friends had hit

the monster, they had also torn a massive hole in the gallery above the Small Hall. In particular, the bust of Lord Defreeque had been blown to smithereens, and while I was ever so sad to lose my favourite perching spot of all, it had revealed something behind it.

A large cavity, from which was now pouring a steady stream of small but very shiny diamonds.

I couldn't believe my eyes at first.

I flew over to make sure, and yes, it was true. The fabulous lost treasure had been found at last.

'ARRRRRRRKKKKK!' I cried, in the longest single syllable I have ever said.

Everyone looked, and then there was

absolute silence, as the truth of the matter sank in.

Solstice said the only thing that anyone could say.

'Gasp!'

There was a long and even more silent silence.

'Edgar,' whispered Solstice eventually. 'You've done it! We're saved! Aren't we, Father? Does this mean we won't have to move?'

Valevine wandered over to the pile of diamonds spilling onto the rug underneath the secret hiding place of the treasure.

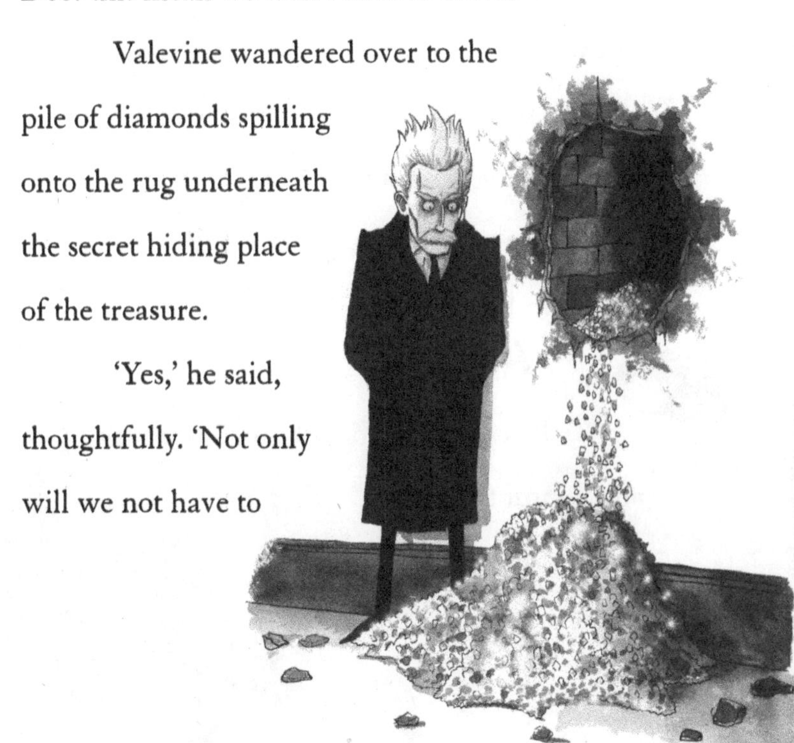

'Yes,' he said, thoughtfully. 'Not only will we not have to

move, I think we can afford to give the place a lick of paint here and there, too. And I think it very possible I will never have to work another day in my life.'

No change there then, but it was not a time for mean thoughts. It was a time for celebration.

And celebrate we did.

We had a party like no other party, and just for once, as I sat with the Otherhands, with all their stupidity and silly ways and strange thoughts, I felt like a very lucky bird.

I turned to Rob, my new little friend, and I had this to say to him.

'Awk?'

It seemed we thought the same way about most things.

'**Erk**,' he said. '**Erk**.'

What could I do but agree?

Erk, indeed, Rob. Erk.

Of course, the castle was not quite as it had been before. Many of the strange things that the space-time vortex had created had not disappeared, but no one seemed too worried that you had to speak your sentences backwards in Valevine's lab, or that the music room stayed upside down, or that it's always snowing in the gallery above the Small Hall.

The castle's always been a little bit different from other homes, after all.

Postscript

Of course, there were still those three bank managers left to visit us and, when they did, they were really very grumpy that we had come up with the cash at the last minute. Quite put out, they were. Well, funnily enough, just as they were being difficult, Nanny Lumber made her appearance in the Small Hall. Now it's a funny thing, that such a small and tiny little lady should be so utterly terrifying, but that's just how she is, and when Minty suggested that the three bank managers might like to sit with her for a while and discuss it all over a cup of tea, they suddenly announced that they needed to be somewhere else.

Bless Nanny Lumber! And that's not something I'd ever thought I'd hear myself say, but then that's the way with life in Castle Otherhand. Always something new to look forward to.

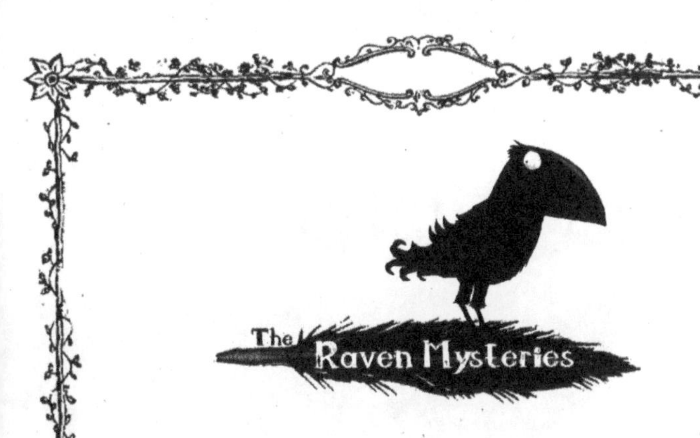

Is my beak wonky? Am I going grey? At the very least I suspect I may have fleas again.

But no matter, I, Edgar, Guardian of the Castle, long-standing protector of the endlessly stupid Otherhand family, and fine example of ravens everywhere, am proud to present this most wonderful piece of modern technology. Not another useless invention from his Lordship, I hear you ask? No, this actually works.

To find out more about The Raven Mysteries books, read my blog, explore the Castle, meet the family, search for the lost treasure of Otherhand, and much more, visit . . .

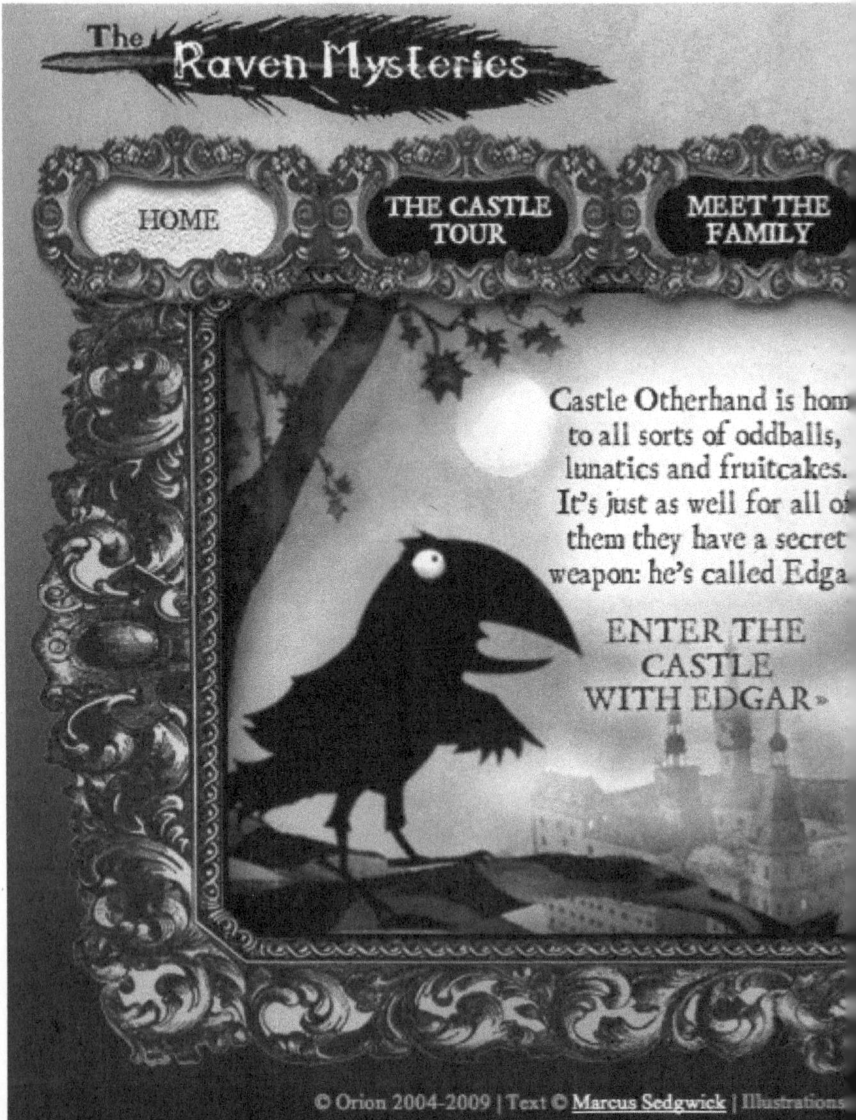
The Raven Mysteries
HOME
THE CASTLE TOUR
MEET THE FAMILY
Castle Otherhand is hom
to all sorts of oddballs,
lunatics and fruitcakes.
It's just as well for all o
them they have a secret
weapon: he's called Edga
ENTER THE CASTLE WITH EDGAR»
© Orion 2004-2009 | Text © Marcus Sedgwick | Illustrations
Terms and conditions | Site

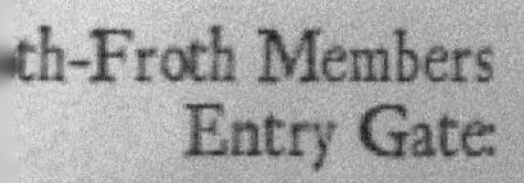

TURN
SOUND
ON

BOOKS
AND AUDIO

GOTH-
FROTH

AUTHOR &
EVENTS

VISIT THE
CASTLE
CLASSROOM!

GO

LATEST BOOK
'LUNATICS
AND
LUCK'

FIND OUT
MORE

ELLAH
'S EDGAR
GAME
or registered
Goth-Froth fans only!

LOG-IN
TO PLAY

LUNATICS
AND LUCK

on | Music © Peter Rinne | Site design by HyperlaunchDMG
Goth-Froths on Facebook